G R JORDAN

Dormie Five

A Highlands and Islands Detective Thriller

First edition

ISBN: 978-1-915562-29-6

This book was professionally typeset on Reedsy.
Find out more at reedsy.com

To find a man's true character, play golf with him.

P.G. WODEHOUSE

Contents

Foreword	iii
Acknowledgement	iv
Novels by G R Jordan	v
Chapter 01	1
Chapter 02	10
Chapter 03	22
Chapter 04	31
Chapter 05	41
Chapter 06	50
Chapter 07	59
Chapter 08	69
Chapter 09	79
Chapter 10	89
Chapter 11	99
Chapter 12	108
Chapter 13	118
Chapter 14	128
Chapter 15	137
Chapter 16	148
Chapter 17	158
Chapter 18	167
Chapter 19	175
Chapter 20	184
Chapter 21	193

Chapter 22	203
Chapter 23	211
Chapter 24	219
Chapter 25	228
Read on to discover the Patrick Smythe series!	235
About the Author	238
Also by G R Jordan	240

Foreword

The events of this book, while based on golf courses in the Inverness area, are entirely fictional and all characters do not represent any living or deceased person.

Acknowledgement

To Ken, Jean, Colin, Evelyn, John and Rosemary for your work in bringing this novel to completion, your time and effort is deeply appreciated.

Novels by G R Jordan

The Highlands and Islands Detective series (Crime)

1. Water's Edge
2. The Bothy
3. The Horror Weekend
4. The Small Ferry
5. Dead at Third Man
6. The Pirate Club
7. A Personal Agenda
8. A Just Punishment
9. The Numerous Deaths of Santa Claus
10. Our Gated Community
11. The Satchel
12. Culhwch Alpha
13. Fair Market Value
14. The Coach Bomber
15. The Culling at Singing Sands
16. Where Justice Fails
17. The Cortado Club
18. Cleared to Die
19. Man Overboard!
20. Antisocial Behaviour
21. Rogues' Gallery
22. The Death of Macleod - Inferno Book 1

23. A Common Man - Inferno Book 2
24. A Sweeping Darkness - Inferno Book 3
25. Dormie 5
26. The First Minister - Past Mistakes Book 1
27. The Guilty Parties - Past Mistakes Book 2
28. Vengeance is Mine - Past Mistakes Book 3

Kirsten Stewart Thrillers (Thriller)

1. A Shot at Democracy
2. The Hunted Child
3. The Express Wishes of Mr MacIver
4. The Nationalist Express
5. The Hunt for 'Red Anna'
6. The Execution of Celebrity
7. The Man Everyone Wanted
8. Busman's Holiday
9. A Personal Favour
10. Infiltrator

The Contessa Munroe Mysteries (Cozy Mystery)

1. Corpse Reviver
2. Frostbite
3. Cobra's Fang

The Patrick Smythe Series (Crime)

1. The Disappearance of Russell Hadleigh
2. The Graves of Calgary Bay
3. The Fairy Pools Gathering

Austerley & Kirkgordon Series (Fantasy)

1. Crescendo!
2. The Darkness at Dillingham
3. Dagon's Revenge
4. Ship of Doom

Supernatural and Elder Threat Assessment Agency (SETAA) Series (Fantasy)

1. Scarlett O'Meara: Beastmaster

Island Adventures Series (Cosy Fantasy Adventure)

1. Surface Tensions

Dark Wen Series (Horror Fantasy)

1. The Blasphemous Welcome
2. The Demon's Chalice

Chapter 01

J enny Maggert half leant on her putter at the edge of the green, staring across at the diminutive Sandra Wu, her opponent in today's match. Sandra stood only five feet tall, but there was power in that compact shape and when she swung a golf club, she opened her shoulders like no one else. Jenny was almost a foot taller than she. A completely different build, having been lanky from secondary school, and now she hoped, having reached the grand age of forty, she was elegant, no longer a pale beanpole.

The fourteenth hole at Newtonmoray's new parkland course was a long par five and yet both women had managed to reach the green in three. Jenny was on the edge of the green and had putted up close, but Sandra, with a nifty seven iron had left herself an eight-foot putt. It was still reasonably early in the morning, probably just after eleven and the two ball had raced out in an effort to get ahead of any other golfers.

This was a match in the ladies' shield, a match-play competition competed for every year and which Jenny had previously won three times. She was by no means a scratch golfer, but in single figures, impressive considering they usually played on the links course which had been the mainstay

1

of Newtonmoray for over one hundred years. Sandra Wu, arriving at the club less than three years ago, had achieved in the space of those three years, a reduction of over twenty in her handicap. Maybe she had been getting lessons from the pro. Jenny wasn't sure, but there was plenty in Sandra's game that said she'd had plenty of instruction.

Although they were in the middle of a parkland course with its young but large trees, specifically brought in and added to what forest had been there before, they were also close to the sea. You could still hear the seagulls from the other course, but there were also birds now nesting around them that you never heard on the other course. The twitters and the warbles from those that preferred a branch to the sand of the beach.

Jenny sniffed the air as she waited for Sandra to line up the putt. It was fresh, woody, like mulch, which was not surprising considering the amount of work that had been done on the course and the amount of added bark suppressing various growing weeds and mosses.

She watched Sandra roll the putt forward and for a moment Jenny held her breath. At the last second the ball rolled to the left, missing the cup by what could only be called millimetres, and settling a foot beyond it. Sandra gave a shake of her head, walked over, and tapped the ball in before picking it out and then finding the flag to replace it into the hole.

'Half in five,' said Jenny, and Sandra nodded before they both removed their scorecards noting down each other's scores as well as their own. The match was still tied with four holes to go. Jenny had taken an early lead but Sandra pulled her back, and now, as the two women pushed their trolleys up the hill to the fifteenth there was a tense air between them. Everything was polite, of course; after all, you couldn't get angry at your opponent. But amidst the woodland that was resplendent in a cold and crisp but beautiful morning, Jenny could feel the tension running through her veins. Her hands weren't quite shaking but they were starting to. These next four holes would decide it. These next four holes would say if Jenny was heading to the semi-final.

The next hole up was the picturesque fifteenth, Sandy's Folly. Jenny thought of the name given by the chairman of the club in a little bit of angst towards the secretary of the club, Sandy Mackintosh. They'd seen Sandy teeing off before them when they were in the car park getting ready. He was on his own and had moved a few holes ahead for Jenny and Sandra were taking their time; after all, this was a competition. Sandy was only out for his morning round, as he often did, and they could see him occasionally knocking two balls along instead of one or he'd pull a shot back to hit it again. *He'd be well ahead now, probably finished*, Jenny thought, and then tried to bring herself back to thinking about the match.

The fifteenth had a tee box that dropped down over a lake onto a green with surrounding bunkers. Just at the edge of the green was a stone structure, a little folly. It had no history. It hadn't been there before the course was built, but the Club Chairman had decided that it was worth the expense to put it in. Mainly because Sandy Mackintosh had vehemently objected to the new course. Jenny was a bit more liberal, though she could see his point. The old course at Newtonmoray had stood for over one hundred years and was well renowned in the area. But this being the north of Scotland, there were plenty of links courses, some with a greater heritage.

Devoid of trees and by the sea, affected by coastal breezes

and variable weather, links courses were seen as proper golf, as it should be played. The new parkland course was more in the modern style, set up for target golf, lacking the intricacies of the more traditional form. Or so critics argued.

The club wanted to step out from just being one of many in the local circuit and had hired a smart new publicity officer. Over the last number of years, they'd gone hook, line, and sinker to sell this new course they'd built. It was certainly challenging and with some modifications, it could probably be brought up to a standard that would challenge the true pro. But to do that, they needed to know that the tour was going to come because then they'd have the ticket sales, and could plan the investment. From what Jenny heard, it was hotly debated in the club's boardroom whether this was the right course for the club.

Mackintosh had objected to all that. He was one of the seven board members, a club secretary for so very long, and a man who liked tradition. She found it funny he was even on the parkland course today, but she'd heard they had closed some of the greens on the links due to a heavy rainfall the previous day. A few of them weren't draining properly and Sandy probably thought he was doing his bit by playing on the 'other course' as he described it.

As they climbed the hill, Sandra Wu suddenly stopped. Jenny thought she winced.

'You okay?' asked Jenny politely.

'The knee,' said Sandra. 'It's just the knee; it's a touch sore. Just give me a minute.'

She sat down on the ground, pulled up her beige trousers, and began to rub at her leg. Jenny found it hard not to get smug at this, her opponent having an injury. She reminded herself she needed to concentrate on her own game. Besides, she was too sporting to try and push Sandra on and instead stood and waited.

'I'll be all right,' said Sandra. But once she had stood up, Jenny noticed how she continued to limp up the hill. The woman was nothing if not a battler and Jenny wondered just how the injury would affect her game. The path up to the fifteenth was one of the steepest on the course, which was reasonably flat, its complexity being in how the holes were shaped. At times, it was skirting along rock land, other times, bending around tall trees that often overhung the fairway.

Because of her opponent's injury, Jenny was looking more at Sandra and less ahead at the path, and it came as a surprise when they arrived at the crest of the path that someone was still on the fifteenth tee. There was a golf bag still inside its trolley sitting just off the tee. Someone seemed to be hunched over a driving club in a rather awkward fashion, the handle of the club seemed thrust in towards their belly. Yet they were perfectly still.

The two women stopped immediately, kept silent, and waited for the player to strike the ball. Jenny assumed there was a ball on the tee thinking it was obscured by the head of the driver.

Driver's a strange choice of club thought Jenny. She didn't know of anybody who really hit a driver here. The hole was a par three one hundred and sixty-odd yards, and for Jenny, it was maybe a good six iron, but to hit a driver at one hundred and sixty yards, you'd need to be a three-year-old, or someone who got so old that there was no power in their limbs at all.

Jenny stood patiently. After ten seconds of the player not moving, she glanced over at Sandra. Sandra looked back with a slight concern on her face. The pair stood perfectly still for another ten seconds then Jenny gave a polite cough. Again, no movement from the player. He was male but because of the low sun coming at them, he was very much in silhouette. There had only been Sandy Mackintosh ahead of them, but Sandy would be finished by now, surely.

Jenny looked at Sandra again and the Asian woman began to walk forward with her trolley. She gave a cough and announced, 'Excuse me, are you okay? Hello.'

Jenny immediately followed suit and the two women approached the tee box, realising that the person was neither answering nor moving. Their golf trolleys were left behind and they approached slowly, aware that something wasn't quite right.

As they reached the tee box, the sun was low behind the trees and the silhouette changed as colour flooded the scene. It was Sandy Mackintosh; Jenny recognised him immediately.

The top of his body seemed to be hanging impossibly, like something was wrong with him. She saw that the driver was pressing into the ground, meaning it didn't slip and Sandy's body was toppled against it, supported just above the waist. Propped up in this fashion, the top half of his body should have collapsed over, but another club had been put down his back. An iron, of which she could see the head beside his neck.

'Dear God,' said Jenny. 'What's . . . is he all right? Is he . . .'

Sandra Wu rushed forward and then stepped back, repulsed. 'He's been knifed, or he's been cut somehow. He's been . . .'

'Is he still alive?' shouted Jenny. Suddenly the blood was racing through her veins. Terror was racing up her back. Somebody dead on a golf course, cut with a knife, slashed?

'Help me,' said Sandra. The smaller woman was pushing

Sandy up off the driver club, which then fell to the floor. As Jenny got close, she could see the slash wounds and the blood across Sandy Mackintosh's chest. More than that, there was copious blood and most of it seemed to emanate from around the neck area. However, with the head flopped over now, Jenny couldn't see what cut had been made.

Sandra was having difficulty supporting the man and Jenny raced in pushing upward as well, but she made too much of an effort, and Sandy rocked back on his heels, the body toppling backwards, collapsing over the top of the little tee box marker that was behind him.

Sandra dropped to her knees, wincing as she did so, but checked the man's neck before listening for any breathing.

'I'll start CPR,' said Sandra.

'Is he dead?' asked Jenny. 'Is he dead?' she shrieked.

'Get a hold of yourself,' said Sandra. 'I'm a nurse, I'll get on this. Get help.'

The words seem to fly past Jenny as she stared at Sandy Mackintosh's neck. It had been sliced, blood splashed all around it. She saw Sandra's hands, now red, even the glove she was wearing, and her white golf shoes were now splattered in crimson.

'I said get help. Get your phone. Ring. Get me some help.'

Jenny didn't move. This couldn't be happening. This wasn't right. She was . . .

Sandra got up from Sandy Mackintosh and physically shook Jenny. 'I know it's scary, I know. I know. What you need to do is get help, get your phone. If the phone's not working, run for the club. Get me help.'

Jenny turned, reached down into her golf bag, unzipped a pocket, and fumbled with her phone. *No bloody signal. No bloody signal.* She turned and began to run. The fifteenth wasn't that far from the clubhouse. The sixteenth went up one way, the seventeenth returned. If she was sensible, she could cut across, past those two, and straight up the eighteenth.

She tore off down a path that bypassed the two holes and found herself coming out at the tee box on the eighteenth. One of the ground staff was there with a grass-cutting machine, mowing back and forward across the tee box. This wasn't unusual for they kept them nice and trim. Jenny waved at the man frantically. He had his head down, ear protectors on, and was happily cutting the grass until he suddenly looked up and saw her standing in front of him.

'What the hell?' he shouted.

It was one of the younger lads. Jeff? Ian? She couldn't remember.

'I need help, I need help. Sandy Mackintosh, he's . . . he's been stabbed!'

'Stabbed, what do you mean?' asked the man on the lawnmower.

'I mean somebody stabbed him. Sandra's with him. Sandra's working on him. I need an ambulance. I need help.'

The man's face went white and then he pointed back the way Jenny had come.

'You go help her. I'll get the ambulance. I'll get the ambulance.'

He jumped off the lawnmower and started sprinting up the eighteenth fairway. Jenny turned and tried running back to Sandra but found that her lungs just wouldn't work. She was out of breath, unsure whether it was from being unfit or simply because the situation was taking her breath from her.

As she ran along, she stopped suddenly, turned to one of

the nearby patches of grass and promptly threw up. *They'd cut his throat, his throat.* Wiping the sick from her mouth with the back of her hand, she turned and ran on, before arriving back at the fifteenth tee. Sandra Wu was working on top of Sandy Mackintosh, her golfing clothes covered in blood. As she continued to work. Jenny stared on in disbelief.

'Is he . . . is he going to be okay?'

Sandra didn't stop but the tears streamed down from her eyes as she fought to continue the rhythm and pace of her work, and told Jenny all she needed to know. Sandy Mackintosh was dead. More than that, Sandy Mackintosh had been murdered.

Chapter 02

Hope McGrath was not in the best of moods. Her partner, John, was off to a conference in London and would be gone for most of the week. She didn't begrudge him it, as he didn't go away much with work, and she was the one always late home or having to stay at the office to complete cases. That was really the difference between being a police detective and a man who ran a car-hire firm.

However, she'd waved him goodbye this morning and wasn't looking forward to time alone in their flat. Should she get Jona to come over at some point? Jona seemed to be more distant these days than she had been in the past. Hope guessed that was normal. After all, life was full of John now, not so much her friends. She'd also been working hard as she was going to step up from a detective sergeant to a detective inspector, and she wanted to make sure she cut the grade.

Seoras Macleod, her boss, was now acting detective chief inspector, and during this interim period while the station sorted itself out, Hope was glad that they hadn't had anything resembling a complex murder. There'd been a few deaths to investigate, but none of them were particularly suspicious, and they were just covering off what needed to be done. She had smartened up her appearance, arriving in a pair of beige trousers with sandy brown boots and a beige jumper, but she couldn't let the leather jacket go. As she hung it on the peg of the interior office, she caught Ross looking at her.

Seoras had moved upstairs to the DCI's office, or rather his office. He had told Hope to move into his former room, the small office that sat inside the main murder team office, but Hope was finding that difficult. She'd always been in amongst the team, never moved to one side like Macleod had been. But he had insisted, said that when things were happening, she would need the peace and the quiet, albeit she could still watch over the team.

'Are you wanting coffee, boss?' asked Ross.

'No, we're not starting that. You're not going to treat me like you treated him in there.'

'He's not in there,' said Ross suddenly. 'If you're going to be his level, I will treat you as I treat him.'

Ross seemed to get much more agitated these days. She thought it was because he was more tired now that they'd finally given Angus and him custody of their own child. It'd been a great day when the whole team had gone round to the house, but Hope wondered if she ever really wanted children. The child had got in her face every time she held him. She just had no motherly instinct. Ross showed more motherly instinct. How'd that work?

'Where's Clarissa?' asked Hope.

'You're worse than him, checking up. I'm here. I'm not late. I'm on time.'

'I wasn't checking up. I just asked where you were,' said Hope.

'I'm right here and I'm going to answer that phone right now.'

11

The main phone of the office was ringing and normally, Ross would race to pick it up, but Clarissa had stormed in, wearing her trademark shawl in a determined fashion to prove that she was not slacking and was in fact on the ball this morning.

'It's Detective Urquhart,' she said, turning and smiling at Hope, and then her face suddenly went grim.

'The golf club,' said Clarissa into the phone. 'Newtonmoray. Who's out there?'

Hope watched Clarissa start writing on a pad of paper, and she glanced at Ross. He was similarly grim-faced.

'Murder? Slashed, you think. Seal it off. Make sure they seal it off. I don't know how you seal off a complete golf course but seal it off.' The phone went down. 'Hope, we've got a dead body at Newtonmoray Golf Club, apparently been slashed, found this morning by two female golfers. Ambulance has been out, confirmed he is dead. By the sounds of what they were saying, there wasn't much they could do. Uniform is out, sealing off as best they can. I suggest we get out there straight away.'

Hope turned and grabbed her jacket from the hanger behind her. 'Ross, give Jona a shout. See everybody outside in five minutes. Grab whatever we need. I'm going upstairs to see Seoras.'

She turned on her heel and marched out of the door. She was in a funny situation as she was still a detective sergeant and DI Macleod had moved up to cover the DCI position, at least temporarily with the idea that it would become permanent. Hope wasn't yet an acting DI. Macleod was covering both roles, and so she did what she would normally do and marched off to see him.

As she approached the office upstairs, she could hear voices inside. She rapped the door in a very formal fashion and waited to be called in.

'Come in,' said Macleod's dulcet tones. She opened the door to see him sitting behind a desk with two people in front of him. She wasn't sure who they were, but she was sure they were more to do with staff issues than actual police work.

'Hope,' said Macleod, smiling, as if he'd been set free from some torture chamber. 'What can I do for you?'

'We've got a body, Seoras, at Newtonmoray Golf Club. Slashed—it looks like murder. Got the team meeting in five minutes outside.'

Macleod looked over at the people in front of him. 'Unfortunately, I have to take this meeting. Our two friends here won't be back up this way for another month. Get on out, sort it, and I'll be there as soon as I can. You know what you're doing, Hope. Just get on top of it and I'll see you shortly.'

Hope could see the grimace in his face, knowing that Macleod would rather run out the door telling whoever these people were to stick it until next month. She guessed there must be other functions he had to fulfil now beyond investigating.

Hope was outside and jumping into her car when Ross gave her a tut. 'No, no, I drive,' he said.

'I'm not DI, I'm still the DS. I'm still your boss and I'm going to drive,' said Hope.

'The boss isn't here. Anything comes through, you have to be able to talk. You can't talk and drive at the same time. That's the way he does it. He does it for a reason.'

'I know he does it for a reason and you can stop talking to me like that. You're awful uppity since you got that kid.'

'That kid's got a name,' said Ross.

13

Right then, Hope couldn't think what the child was called. She was hoping to put Ross back in his box, hoping to put a little bit of emphasis on the fact that he was not being normal but instead, she was going to give the message that the most important thing in Ross's life didn't mean much to her. She picked the keys out of the ignition, stepped out, and threw them to him.

'All right, you drive, but keep this up and I'll be going in that little green sports car.'

Clarissa was giving a wave, as some poor unsuspecting constable got in the car beside her. Hope doubted they would reach the golf course before Clarissa because Ross was a much smoother, and dare she say it, more sensible driver.

The golf course was out to the east from Inverness along the shores of the Moray firth, and she remembered it from interest the papers had taken in it over the last lot of years. They had a new course built there.

Hope wasn't a golfer. She'd never seen much point, hitting the ball around with a stick. She'd much rather go for a run, much rather be in the gym, working things out, building up a bit of a sweat. Maybe when she was older. Or was it bowls you did at that age, or something else? Walking. Get a dog. She wasn't ready for anything like that.

It took about thirty minutes to get out to the golf club and when they joined the small road that led up to the clubhouse, Hope could see the two distinct parts of the grounds. To her left was rolling green, with the sea beyond, while to her right, an enclosure of trees.

'It's pretty amazing, isn't it?' said Ross.

'What do you mean?' asked Hope.

'It's pretty amazing. You've got a links course on your left and you've got this parkland course on your right. The fact they're so close together and they're so very different. Having seen them both, I do like the new one, I have to say.'

'Having seen them both? When do you play golf?'

'Oh, I caddy now and then for Angus. He quite enjoys it. I haven't been out on the course with him since Junior arrived though. Takes up quite a bit of time.' Ross negotiated the police cars that were there and the reporters' cars that had arrived. There was a cordon into the golf club car park and Hope flashed her warrant card, but it seemed completely unnecessary as one of the local constables waved them in with a nod. Hope could see that Jona's waggon was here. There seemed to be little activity around it. As she stepped out to the car, she grabbed hold of a nearby constable.

'Who's in charge of the scene?' she asked.

'Sergeant Halford. He's down at the body now. He's given instructions that we're to keep here clear. We've also had some of the board coming in.'

'And where are they going?' asked Hope.

'Well, we allowed them into the clubhouse.'

'Has anyone cordoned off the lockers?' asked Ross.

The constable shook his head.

'Sergeant,' said Ross, 'we should close off the lockers. If someone's been murdered out there and they're a golfer, they may have gone to the lockers beforehand or have been coming back to them.'

Hope dispatched Ross to do so and then called the recently arrived Clarissa to her. As they walked down to the fifteenth tee, a member of the ground staff escorted them and then stood well back as Hope saw the tape that marked Jona's domain. Instead of moving inside the cordon, she waited for Jona to

15

step out.

'What have you got for me?' asked Hope.

'Male, into his seventies. Apparently, he's called Sandy Mackintosh. I think they said he was the club secretary. Anyway, he was found by two women. Said he was propped up on a golf club. So, the driver, that's the long club, was up into his belly, keeping him upright so it looked like he was ready to take a shot. There was another golf club down his back keeping him more upright, but the women obviously didn't know what condition he was in. When they went to assist, they removed the front club, tried to push him backwards and he fell over.

'Then Miss Sandra Wu, one of the women who found him, a nurse, began CPR. He's been slashed across the chest, but I believe that what killed him is the slash across the neck. Blood all down his front. Getting to work on it.'

Jona sounded out of breath. It was cold and crisp, with a real chill to the March air.

'Trying to preserve the scene to see if there's any footprints but we're in the middle of a golf course, Hope. People walk up and down here all the time. I'll try and search and see what we can find. We'll cover the area around here, but the knife is a serious knife and the cut seems to be quite well done.'

'Okay,' said Hope, 'I'll get out of your hair. Dig me out what you can. I think it's time to start rounding up some golfers and to find out just who this guy was.' Clarissa returned with Hope to the clubhouse where they met Ross.

'Well, it's not a pretty sight,' said Hope. 'Let's make sure we're on top of this. Jona is dealing with the scene. We'll let her get on with it and see what she comes up with. We've got our deceased man, Sandy Mackintosh, Club Secretary. We need to find out about him. Also need to interview our two women who found him.'

'Sandra Wu, and a Jenny Maggert,' said Ross instantly.

'Thank you, Ross. You and I will do that shortly. Ross, make sure that Jona is finished with them, though, in case there's any of their clothing she needs. I need also to talk to someone in charge of this place.'

'Alastair Begley, Club Chief Operating Officer,' said Ross. Hope was astonished as ever. They could only have been away less than half an hour and the man knew everything about the place. 'He's up in a boardroom. I can take you there directly.'

'Who else would've been out and about here? It's a golf club. I'm not sure how it works,' she said. She glanced over at Ross.

'Need to see who was out on the course,' he said. 'Would need to know who teed off. Probably the best people to talk to would be the grounds people. They're out most days cutting greens, trimming up the rough, doing bits of work here and there. They'd have been out in the early morning as well because it gets busy in the afternoon, harder to do the job. I think we should go and talk to them.'

'Where would they be?' asked Hope.

Ross looked around. 'See the large shed in the distance. That looks like a good bet,' he said. 'Do you want me to talk to them?'

'No,' said Hope. 'Clarissa, you have a great touch with the common people, don't you?'

Clarissa glared at her. 'I did play golf in the past.'

'Good,' said Hope. 'You'll be talking their language. You're on the ground staff. Ross, take me to this Chief Operating Officer and then get back with our two witnesses.'

Ross took Hope into the golf club. As she walked along, she

17

stared through open doors. It was all wooden panels in the rooms and carpets that were plush. Hope reckoned it must cost a fortune to belong to something like this, and when she was led into a boardroom with a large table and seven seats, she was astonished at the number of photographs along the walls. There was a man sitting down at the table and he stood up, offering his hand.

'This is Alastair Begley, the Club Chief Operating Officer,' said Ross. Hope nodded, thanked Ross, dismissed him, and then stepped over to Alastair Begley, taking his hand and shaking it.

'I'm sorry for your loss,' said Hope, 'but I would like to know a little bit about this place.' They were beside a large window and Hope noted that snow had started to fall. Jona wouldn't be impressed. 'Just who is Sandy Mackintosh?' she asked.

'Well, at this club,' he said, 'we have a board that consists of seven people. Sandy was one of those people, the Club Secretary. I am the Club Chief Operating Officer. We've got Club Chairman, a Deputy Chairman. We've got a Publicity and Promotions Director, though that's been fairly recent, we've also got a Staff Manager, and we've got a Golf Operations Manager. That's who runs the club.'

'Had Mr Mackintosh been here long?' asked Hope.

'Sandy was a fixture here. Sandy had been here since . . . ooh, I think he joined the board when he was about thirty.'

'Had been in the Club Secretary role all that time?'

'No, he used to cover publicity and promotions in his role as the Club Manager, as it was called back then. It was less about marketing and more about making sure the place stayed afloat. The titles have always changed but there's always been seven running the club. Sandy has been one of them for a long time.'

'Has there been any friction around what Sandy has been doing, given that he's been likely murdered?'

'Well,' said Begley looking rather sheepish. 'There certainly has been. Where Sandy was found, that's the new course, our beloved parkland Course. We built that ten years ago and at the time when it was happening, Sandy was dead against it. I was too. We're Scottish here—links golf is golf, the correct golf.'

Hope looked at him blankly. 'Links golf?'

'When you came in, you probably saw two courses, one here where you see the woods but if you go down to the other path and you can see out the window over there, it's the . . .'

'The course without trees,' said Hope.

'Yes,' said Begley a little bit patronisingly, 'the course without trees. It's coastal. You get the benefit of all the wind changes, the sea breezes. It's more of a challenge. It's proper golf; it's what it was designed for.'

'But you built this other one?'

'Yes, but more than that, you see the more American course, the parkland one, was the dream of some of our newer people. A lot of people at clubs now want the image and want the club to be talked about. Sandy was traditional; he wanted things done properly, not all about image. It's not about the numbers of people coming. But other people don't see it that way.

'Like most clubs, we've suffered financially; it hasn't been easy. The bigger more American-style courses seem to attract people, richer people, and if we can entice them to play, we can get more money into the club—this was their argument. More than that, if we can actually get a course that is part of a tour event that people come into to watch the pros in, they'll want to play that course. You can charge more; you can get more high-paying visitors, instead of club members.'

'Sandy didn't like that?'

'Sandy was against it in so many ways,' said Alastair Begley. 'To be frank, I am too, but this is my job, it's what I do. It is funny though, where he was killed.'

'Funny?' said Hope. 'Why?'

'The fifteenth on the new course, it's called Sandy's Folly. It's ostensibly a tribute to him for all he's done at the club. There's a little concrete shed-like thing at the back of the green and they called it a folly. It's not a real folly, though, and they named it Sandy's Folly, but what it really was intended to say was that you were wrong, Sandy.

'Weird that Sandy was even playing that course but then again, the greens are off today; there's trouble on the links course. Sandy doesn't like to play the links course unless it's fully open. He probably went down on the new one so he could get back into the clubhouse and complain about it.'

'You spoke about the fact that you wanted to get pro golfers here, tournaments, I think. That's what you were getting at. Have you had any success with that?'

'Well, that's been the big thing at the moment. They've almost got a deal, but it's got to go through the board. You see around here, there's always been seven people on the board; the names and the positions may change but there's always been seven. In the constitution of this club, you have to get a dormie five.'

'A what?' queried Hope.

'Dormie five. In golf, when you're up by so many holes in a match and there's only that many holes left, you can't lose the match, you could only draw, so the term is dormie. Here, you can't lose when you have five out of seven voting in your favour, so it's called a dormie five. The dormie five is how this club has worked. The problem those who want to bring in the pros have, is they don't have dormie five. They're not even close.'

The door opened and a small woman walked in, announcing to Mr Begley that the press were looking for a statement from him.

'Do you mind if I make a statement?' the man asked Hope.

'No, but don't comment on the case. Tragic regret that your friend has died; assisting the police in every way we can. Nothing more. If they ask you about what you think has caused the man's death, you say nothing. Police are investigating; refer them to us.'

'Understood,' said Begley. 'If you'll excuse me.'

He walked out of the room and Hope continued to stare out of the window. It was true you could see the new course and the old course. Clearly, there was more at play here than a simple golfing accident. It was unclear to her why somebody would want to kill him. Maybe she wouldn't need Macleod on this one; maybe this one would be quick and easy. *Aye, Hope*, she thought, *when has that ever happened?*

Chapter 03

With the assistance of Sergeant Halford, Clarissa managed to round up the ground staff that were working that morning. They'd all gathered back in a large shed, which contained their mowers and other vehicles. At one end was a large urn and tea was being made and passed out. The course was big, and with being two courses as well, Clarissa reckoned there'd be numerous staff to keep it in good shape.

'My name's Detective Sergeant Clarissa Urquhart, over from Inverness. You're all probably aware of what's happened today. In case you're not, Sandy Mackintosh was found on the fifteenth tee of your new course, deceased. I'm not here to accuse any of you of anything. I'm just here to try and find out who was about this morning, who you may have seen, and if you saw anything unusual. We'll be trying to trace Sandy's steps and trying to find out a little bit about the club. Now, before we start, can I have one of those?' Clarissa pointed to the mugs that were being passed around.

'Jimmy,' said an older man, 'get the officer one. How do you like it?'

'I actually like coffee,' said Clarissa, 'but if it's going to be tea, make it strong. A little bit of milk.'

'You heard her,' said the man. 'My name is Frank Macleod. I'm the head groundskeeper. I can help you with any of the team here, when they were on, when they arrived, what their assignments were for today. Just take it easy. We all knew Mackintosh, good old soul.'

Clarissa nodded and took a cup of tea in hand. Although she was standing in her shawl and inside the shed, it was cool and there was an open door at one end through which she could see snow beginning to fall.

The man must have caught her looking at it, for Frank announced, 'Don't worry about that. That's not going to lie. If we thought it was, we'd probably have closed the course. Bit of a change from this morning though. This morning was a cracking morning, cold but bright.'

'Who was out on the course this morning?' asked Clarissa.

'Well, on the new course today, Sandy Mackintosh was the only one out very early, followed by the two women that were playing their competition. Sandra had come and asked me a couple of days previously about the weather. I'd said that there would be snow later in the afternoon, so she would arranged with, I think it's Mrs Maggert, to go out early.'

'Jenny Maggert?' asked Clarissa to clarify.

'That's her. Mrs Maggert and Sandra Woo. They were playing in the Ladies' Shield, so they were out behind.'

'That's right,' said Jimmy. 'I was up near the first tee. Sandy went ahead of them and then it was them.'

'Anybody else see them when they went round?'

There was a bit of chatter amongst them before the ground staff came to the conclusion that the ladies had gradually fallen a little bit behind.

23

'Was anybody up on the fifteenth?' asked Clarissa.

The team looked blankly until Frank spoke. 'Nobody was assigned to go up there. We had sixteen and seventeen in use, but you won't see fifteen from there. We had others out further back. Thirteen was being looked at. Eight and six.'

'You saw Sandy Mackintosh moving ahead of the two ladies following him?'

'Isla said Sandy got to about a half an hour ahead. It wouldn't be surprising a single player on their own. Sandy would motor round. He won't be that interested as it's the new course. He's just doing it because that's what he does. There's nothing to do at the club in the morning in his official role. He'd have come in and gone out and played.'

'Played it to find out something to complain about,' said a girl at the back of the group.

'What's your name?' asked Clarissa.

'Isla,' she said. Clarissa reckoned she could only have been in her early twenties. 'He used to talk to me quite a bit when we were out on the course. He was always complaining about the new course. Never about the work we were doing, just moaning about why was it built. It wasn't this, it wasn't as good as the other course. If you're out on the links with him, he'd be talking about how this hole, and how it compares to the holes back on the new course. Sandy just did not like the new course,' said Isla. 'It's a bit unfair. They are just two different types of courses.'

Frank almost snorted. 'You know that don't cut it here, Isla. Isla is quite new to our contingent, and she's still got to learn about how set in their way some people get. Sandy wouldn't like new people coming. Well, not new people. He wasn't against new people. He was actually quite welcoming to people who joined the club. Yes, he liked to tell them how it worked, et cetera, but he was very supportive of them. If somebody wanted to join and had financial difficulties, he would push to sort it out. He wasn't an unkind person. I don't want you to get the wrong idea,' said Frank.

'But he was very opinionated about the type of course we should have here. I remember back when we went through the debates about getting the new course, the board at the time was split and it was four to three. Sandy was one of the ones against, and then old Johnny died. Sandy was livid when the person who took up the role voted for the new course. First decision, first vote, and it overturned what Sandy had been saying to block the course. You see, at four to three, they could have blocked it. Five to two, that was dormie.'

'Dormie? How does that work with the board?' asked Clarissa.

'Here, you have to vote five to two. If you haven't got a five to two majority, it doesn't pass. That's the way they work it here. Dormie rules. Pain in the neck, trust me, but dormie rules.' Clarissa nodded, and sipped some of her tea.

'The thing is,' said Frank, 'I know you're asking us who we saw today, and like we told you, we saw Sandy, we saw the two ladies behind him. There was a number then starting later in the day, but they would've only reached the fifth on the other side of the course. They wouldn't have been anywhere near Sandy. This course, unlike the links, is so well-hidden. When you're out on the links on the other side, you can see most of the people on it. It's on the side of that hill dropping down to the sea. The holes run back and forward. I mean, there's nowhere to hide out on the links, and it's brutal because of the wind. This course here, we were able to shape it more when it was built. It used some of the features, the terrain, and some of the woods that were there, but you built the holes to be hidden. Be very self-contained. There's little paths disappearing here, there, and everywhere.'

'That's right,' said Isla. 'You could sneak around there, no problem. You can stop here, hide there.'

Clarissa wondered, *Was this a planned attack? How did they know he was going to be there?* 'How well do you have to know these paths?' asked Clarissa. 'Are they obvious?'

'No,' said Frank. 'There are some obvious ones that are signposted, tell you how to cut through to here and there, but no, a lot of the other ones are smaller; they're not even proper paths. They're like sheep runs except we don't have any sheep, obviously. Deer run paths, call it what you will, but it's just a track in the ground, but if you know which ones to look for, and you know where you're going . . .'

'You seem to have quite a contingent of ground staff, Frank. Some of the golf clubs I've been at, they don't have that many.'

'We've got two courses to look after,' said Frank. 'There's also been the drive to get this one up to speed. We've almost got the tour coming here. There was a guy came along, Dermot somebody, and had a look around the course. We had to get it perfect that day. The chairman, Mr Peters, came out with me. He said we did a great job on it, which was really nice because we did; we put a lot of hard work into it.

'That was also what was bugging Sandy, though, because a lot of the work we've been told to do has been on the new course, not on the old course. Sandy used to think that the old course was going to start going to rot because we weren't spending enough time on it. That's not totally true. I know what I'm doing with the old course. She doesn't need that much attention to stay in a decent state. To be in a really good state, like all courses, yes, but my instructions were to focus our time and energy on getting the new one up to standard.

'That's why most of these guys were out there this morning. We had a few on the old course but not many. Most of us are working away here because we have flowers to do. This is the thing they were talking about. When they come with their telly cameras if we get a tour event, the holes have to look good on camera. I mean, I'm a groundsman for a golf course. I have everything set up from the point of view of standing on a tee—what does the golfer see? Where is that ball going to go? How do you trap them? How thick should your rough be? Where does that bunker go? Everything I was thinking about is what the shot looks like to the golfer.

'This Dermot guy came around, and he's talking to me about what it looks like from a camera angle up here and how does this show and how does that show, and where would the people be. Now, if the people are going to be here, we really need a nicer set of flowers along here. He was talking like it was the Augusta National over in America.'

'That's the one with that bridge,' said Clarissa. 'The azaleas?'

'That's it. That's what they were talking about. It sure looks good on the television. I'm sure it looks great over there too. It's made me have to think differently, plant new small trees, bushes, plants. I mean, this is Scotland, so you've got to factor in the weather, what type of plant you want. Sometimes it's just wood chippings that go down here and there. Everything's got to look spot-on; it's got to look good. To the people that come, it's got to look good, on the camera, and you've still got to put up a challenge. It's not easy. Been doing a lot of work with Alastair on it, God help him. He's not that keen. He didn't want the new course to be like this. He wanted the old course because the old course has got the heritage.'

'This is maybe a bit of a long shot,' said Clarissa, 'but is there anybody outside of the golf course that could have gone for Sandy Mackintosh? Did he upset anybody outside of here that you know of?'

'No,' said Frank. 'I mean these guys won't know anything about that. They'll just see Sandy on the course. I mean, he hasn't said anything to anyone, has he?'

'Not really,' said Isla. 'It was bugging him, the new course and the old course, because the chairman, Mr Peters, and him were very, very good friends. I know Sandy talked about when they used to go around to see each other, known each other enough for a long time. It really hurt him that they were divided over this course. It felt strange because in some ways, he said he felt sorry for Mr Peters. I asked him why and he just didn't say anything. That was Sandy, though. There was a very private side to him. Yet, in terms of the club, he expressed what he wanted, at least as far as I could tell in my time here,' said Isla.

'She's right though,' said Frank. 'That's him, always talking about the club, talking about the issues of the club. When you went a little bit more personal, much quieter. Of course, both he and Mr. Peters have lost their wives. Not that long ago for Mr Peters—she got cancer. She only passed in the last couple of weeks. Sandy's died a couple of years ago. Yes, I remember back in the day, you'd have seen them every Saturday night at the club and the ladies with them, at their table together. In fact, I'm sure that they used to play four-ball together at one point, but with the new course, it was quite surprising that they managed to keep that relationship going. Then again, maybe they're sensible like people are.'

'What do you mean?' asked Clarissa.

'This is business. You have disagreements, but that doesn't mean you disagree about things outside of the golf club. Doesn't mean you shouldn't get on with each other, does it?'

'Well, somebody clearly didn't get on with him,' said Clarissa. 'Somebody clearly had an issue.'

'Well, I can't argue with you there,' said Frank. 'Can I ask you something?'

'Of course,' said Clarissa. 'I might not be able to answer though.'

The man nodded thoughtfully, and then said, 'The two women, I mean Sandra Woo and Jenny, they're not under suspicion, are they?'

'I can't say they're under suspicion. I can't say they won't be under suspicion in the future. We've only just arrived. We're gathering information. So far, they are witnesses and the only witnesses we've got. '

'I'll tell you something,' blurted out one of the young lads.

'Jimmy,' said Frank, 'easy.'

'No, no,' said Jimmy. 'Not Jenny, she was upset. I mean, when she came to get me and I ran back up here to raise the alarm, she was upset. Don't even think about anything to do with her. She was upset; she was genuine. '

'Woah,' said Clarissa. 'Easy. Thank you for that. That helps, but we haven't been looking at them from that point of view yet, we're still gathering information. I realise it's going to be quite upsetting, but please, we'll take further statements from you individually. Thank you for now and thanks for the cup of tea,' said Clarissa, handing it back over to Jimmy.

She turned and walked to the edge of the hut and saw the

29

snow now falling much thicker than it was before. 'You said this wasn't going to lie, Frank,' said Clarissa over her shoulder. 'Are you sure about that?'

The groundsman walked up behind her and looked out. 'There's no way that's going to lie,' he said. 'I mean, look at it.'

'It's going to lie on my shoulder,' said Clarissa.

'Do you want a jacket?' he said. She watched him turn around, disappear into the shed, and come back with a large yellow jacket that he draped over her shoulders. 'I'll walk you back over.'

Clarissa saw the outstretched hand of the man indicating she should walk in front of him. He soon joined her side. Now, that's different, she thought. They always say it's a gentlemanly sport, golf, but I never found that when I played. Clarissa gave the man a smile as he escorted her back to the clubhouse.

Chapter 04

Hope normally embraced the initial chaotic scenes around a murder investigation. Yes, there were tried and trusted methods, but there was always a sense of panic from the people around you. There was always the frenzy of the press trying to find out what was going on, and there was always a stack of people to be interviewed and spoken to who had never been involved in a murder investigation. Your colleagues were all veterans. Even most of the constables in uniform had closed off areas for serious reasons, but there was a hurly-burly to it. Usually, Hope felt on the top of that hurly-burly, a centre of calm in the storm.

As early ideas raced through her head, Hope remembered to be quick yet thorough, just in case there was a chance the murderer could be caught because they hadn't cleared the area. As she oversaw the chaos in front of her, Hope spotted the compact figure of Jona Nakamura, the station's forensic lead, and one of her closest friends. She was still wearing her forensic suit, making a beeline towards Hope, which usually meant there was information coming. A constable walked up to Hope, ready to tell her something, but she put her hand up, apologised, and marched towards Jona.

'What is it?'

'Well, hello to you as well,' said Jona. 'You haven't been standing out in the snow, desperately trying to cover up a crime scene.'

'Okay, hello, Jona. Apologies. Now, what is it?'

The Japanese woman smiled and then said, 'Not here,' taking Hope by the arm and dragging her away from the edge of the cordon. She marched over to the clubhouse, walked in through the front door, and demanded from someone where there was a private room.

'Jona, this way. We're operating out there.' A temporary room had been taken and Jona marched into it, throwing herself down on a seat and scanning the room quickly.

'Don't tell me you don't trust the people in here either,' said Hope in a low, hushed voice.

'Of course, I do. Where's the coffee? I'm frozen.'

Hope gave a laugh, turned around and realised that there wasn't one. 'Guess Ross hasn't been in here yet then,' she said, 'but enough of that. What is it?'

'I've been looking at the victim and to be honest with you,' said Jona, 'whoever wielded this blade knew how to use it. The slashes across the chest are not slashes, there're deep cuts that affect major organs, and the cut to the throat is perfection. Right on the spot, just deep enough. The chances of Mackintosh surviving that cut were minimal. You'd have to have a full team around him immediately, close up the wound and intubate. He would have needed a medical team on hand. But the other cuts, I think, were made first because otherwise, they make no sense. Made to almost hold him in his tracks, position him, make sure he didn't get away.'

'Hold him? Why hold him if you're just going to cut his

throat?' asked Hope. 'That doesn't make sense.'

'Well, maybe they wanted to talk to him. Maybe they wanted Sandy Mackintosh to understand why he was being killed. I don't know,' said Jona, 'I just tell you what the scene tells me. One thing's for clear, that's not a normal blade. I'm going to try and identify it for you, but while it's not a normal one, it's a darn effective one. I need to talk to some other people in the field. Maybe they'll have a better idea. In the meantime, we've got to get these lockers searched as well. I take it, we've identified which one was Mr Mackintosh's.'

'Have spoken to the constable down there. He's guarding the door. No one's been in since we've locked it off.'

'Which was when?' asked Jona.

'When I got here,' said Hope. 'Anything else you can tell me about the scene?'

'It's a pretty big area. Where do you want me to concentrate? For now, I'm working around that fifteenth tee, moving out from it. Do I go backwards, round the course? Do we search the whole course? What are we looking at here?'

'I'm waiting for Clarissa to come back, to see if we can trace where Mr Mackintosh went. It's probably going to be by the numbers, holes one to fifteen.'

'Unless he was set up, brought in from somewhere else.'

'I don't think so. From the sounds of it, he was out on the course.'

'I've been looking through the bag as well. The club that was used up his back seems to have been from his bag as was the driver. But the whole idea of making him look like an actual golfer on the tee, what was that all about? Were they trying to say something?'

'I doubt it,' said Hope. 'Probably looking to hold him up

there to get away. That's something else I'm going to need to investigate. I'm just about to go and interview my two witnesses, but I want to talk to Clarissa first. She should be heading this way.'

Almost on cue, Clarissa opened the door before turning around and thanking someone rather loudly. Hope caught a glimpse of a man in a green uniform and a smile on Clarissa's face.

'Did you get somewhere?'

'Do you mean with the case or with the man in the uniform?' asked Jona.

'Get out,' said Hope. 'Go find me something better.' Jona gave a laugh and a big thumbs up to Clarissa, who looked rather bemused as Jona walked out.

'What's up with her?'

'Never mind,' snapped Hope. 'What'd you find out?'

'Okay, easy!'

'Sorry,' said Hope. She took a deep breath. Just as Clarissa went to speak, her phone rang. She picked it up and saw Macleod's name. 'Not you now,' Hope said out loud.

'Seoras?' said Clarissa. 'Switch it off.'

'I can't close the call down. He's the DCI!'

'Of course, you can,' said Clarissa and grabbed Hope's phone and closed the call. Hope shot her a look.

'You need to hear what I have to say first. There's no point answering that call, half telling him what you know and then talking to me and then making a second phone call. If he's annoyed about it, put him my way.'

Hope gave a sigh. 'Just tell me what you found out.'

Clarissa related all that she'd heard from the ground staff, including how the board was extremely divided.

'Well, that's interesting,' said Hope. 'Seems there could be some good reasons for bumping him off.'

'It's all quite heated,' said Clarissa, 'but what's also strange is that Peters, the Club Chairman, and Mackintosh were really good friends and have still been. Both became widows recently, or at least in the last couple of years. Peter more recent.'

Hope took a moment, tried to assess what Clarissa told her, and she looked up at the woman. 'Where's Ross?'

'Don't know,' said Clarissa. 'Is he meant to be doing something for you?'

'He's always doing something. We're going to be interviewing the two witnesses who found the body. Tell you what I need you to do; go and find Begley, the Operations Manager. Tell him I want the board here to talk to them all together. Maybe also individually, but get a hold of the names, the contact numbers, and tell him to pull them all to the clubhouse. We're going to need to find out where they all were today. Clarissa, don't take no for an answer.'

'No for an answer? When have I ever taken no for an answer?'

Clarissa stepped back out of the room, still wearing the fluorescent jacket she'd been given previously, and as she did so, she marched into Ross coming the other direction. Behind him were a couple of waitresses carrying large flasks and cups.

'Als, you're a lifesaver. I got a cup of tea over in the other hut, but it's so cold out there.'

Ross pointed to a table at the side of the room, advising the waitresses to leave the cups and flasks there. Once he'd thanked them, he closed the door behind him. Clarissa was still hanging around, now pouring herself a coffee.

'I said board,' said Hope.

'I'm on my way. I can do it with a coffee!' Clarissa almost danced out of the room, shutting the door behind her, just slightly firmer than she should have.

'Have we got our witnesses ready?'

'Upstairs. I just thought you'd like something to drink in the meantime. You haven't had anything since we've been here.'

'No, I haven't. Thank you.' Ross turned to pour a cup for Hope, but she stopped him.

'Enough, Ross. I'm not Macleod. You don't need to do everything for me. I'm not like him. I don't just use my brain.'

She heard the snigger behind her from one of the constables, turned around, and shot a deadly look at him. Once the man had crawled back under his shell, she turned back to Ross. He was standing with a deadpan face, although she was sure he was laughing behind it.

'What I mean is, I don't just sit and brood on stuff. This is a moment of action.'

'Never said anything,' said Ross.

'Take my cup up. I'll be there in a couple of minutes. I just need to phone the DCI.'

'You can still call him the boss.'

Hope waved her hand, ushering Ross out of the room. She just felt so claustrophobic today. What was up with her? It wasn't like she hadn't run investigations before, or she hadn't been on top of things.

It took her ten minutes to pass on the information to Macleod, and she sat waiting for his advice and instruction of what to do. He advised he would be up shortly once he got rid of his visitors. He was unnerving her. Why wasn't he asking more questions? Why wasn't he firing into this? He used to keep her on her toes. Macleod was a bloodhound when a case came up. Always pushing, always thinking about the different angles, and yet he'd said nothing on the phone.

Hope marched up the stairs and went into a small room where the door was slightly ajar. Once she was inside, Ross closed it behind her, and she saw two women sitting down. One reminded her of Jona, small in stature but who looked in control. Beside her, a white Scottish woman seemed to be trembling a little.

'I'm Detective Sergeant Hope McGrath, in charge of the investigation, and this is Detective Constable Ross. Thank you both for what you've done today. I know this might be hard, but I just want to run through it again, if you're okay with that.'

'Yes.' The Asian woman nodded, but there was no movement from the white woman.

'It's Jenny Maggert and Sandra Wu. I think we know who's who,' said Hope. 'I believe you two were competing against each other.'

'That's right,' said Sandra Wu. 'We had just played fourteen holes. It was all square. We were heading up to the fifteenth. I stopped briefly on the way up the hill to the fifteenth because my leg was sore. When I'd sorted that, I climbed up with Jenny. We then saw this figure on the tee box.'

'Did you know who it was at the time?' asked Hope.

'We knew that Sandy Mackintosh had gone out ahead of us, but we thought he'd be in the clubhouse by then.'

'Why?' asked Hope.

'Because he's on his own. A single golfer can fly around the course much quicker. We were playing a match, taking our time over putts, sorting scorecards out. The reason we were out in the morning was because I checked the weather a few days before. This afternoon was, well, expecting snow. Also, if we got out early in the morning, we wouldn't be in a bunch of those midday people. They can be quite slow. We wanted to be out on our own with plenty of time, not have anyone pushing up behind us. It was important for our match. We're quite competitive.'

'Is that right? Jenny, is it?' said Hope. The woman looked up at her. She was still shaking.

'Forgive me,' said Sandra. 'I'm a nurse. Jenny's in shock. I think she needs to not go home on her own from here. You can take her down to the hospital to be looked at.'

'Okay,' said Hope. 'When you saw the figure, what happened? What did you do?'

'Well, we went up, and he was propped up with the golf club. Jenny froze, and I tried to remove it and then hold him up. Jenny assisted, and we seemed to push him over, and he landed on his back. To be honest, I think he was dead already. I looked at the cuts and I just started CPR. I wanted to see if I could get the heart going. I screamed at Jenny to go and get help. She struggled at first, terrified but she went, and then she came back, and I was covered in blood. She then went into a real panic.'

'Did you see anyone around?' asked Hope.

'No. We'd only seen the greenkeepers when we were out on the course, but we didn't see any of them up ahead of us towards the fifteenth. To be honest, you can get to the fifteenth so easy.'

'That's right,' said Jenny suddenly. 'That's right. Lots of paths. My husband dropped me off there before. Walked up as I was meeting people playing in, accompanying them over the last few holes. Yes, so many paths. You can go anywhere really easy.'

'What happened after that?'

'Well, I kept working,' said Sandra, 'until the paramedics got to me. To be honest, it was pointless. He was gone. I kind of knew it. Pity because he was a good guy for the club even if he didn't like the new course.'

'Are you aware of any issues with the club? Anyone who would have anything against Sandy Mackintosh?'

'Against Sandy Mackintosh?' queried Sandra. 'No. Not against him. He and the Club Chairman were on different sides, but the Club Chairman and the Club Deputy Chair are both on different sides and they get on. I mean, they might argue a bit about golf and things but not outside. Sandy had been here so long. Everyone appreciates what he does, even if they don't always agree with his opinion. Sandy was a good guy.'

'Yes, he was,' said Jenny, suddenly, and she began to cry, putting two hands up to her face. Hope sat and ran the women through the story two more times. She wondered if they had seen anybody at the lockers before their round, but the women had seen nobody. Other than raising the alarm and making a valiant attempt to save the man's life, they seemed to be of little help, especially in establishing who had killed him.

'We'll need to take DNA and fingerprints from you just so we can rule you out from the scene if that's okay with you.'

'That's fine,' said Sandra, 'but seriously, we need to get Jenny some help. It's going to take more than a cup of tea to get her right at the moment.'

'Okay, I'm just going to step outside with DC Ross, and then I'll send him back in to organise all that, okay? But thank you for your time.' Hope and Ross stepped outside into the corridor.

'What's up?' he asked.

'Sort the two women out then get down to the fifteenth, I want to know what paths lead up to it. I want to know where they go, I want to know what CCTV is available around the area. This is ideal for you, Ross. See what people could have been observed and then find me footage of who was observed, particularly be looking out for any of the board members because we know there's a dispute going on there.'

Ross nodded and then went back into the room, leaving Hope on her own. She had wished that talking with the witnesses might have brought something out, but it wasn't so. Macleod will be up soon, and she wanted to show him progress, but at the moment, she was still developing theories about people that might want to kill. In truth, it all seemed very extreme over something where you hit balls around a course with a stick. Sometimes, she didn't understand other people's passions.

Chapter 05

Ross was wrapped up in a large coat with a bobble hat and was wearing a rather smart set of boots he had purchased a few weeks ago for moments such as this. They had fur inside, warm on his feet, and although not the most graceful and certainly not office wear, if you were out on a crime scene, he felt they were unlikely to be beaten.

The last few weeks had been full on for him. With a new child in the house, his partner, Angus, up to high doh, and then all the consternation at work of the boss moving upstairs and Hope not really stepping into the reins of DI yet, Ross was unbalanced. He liked form and function. He liked to know what he had to do, when to do it, and how to do it. He was also missing being there for the inspector.

He had it on good authority that the secretary on the floor above did not make Macleod's coffee correctly. It was something that Ross had prided himself on. During all his time of working with the man, he had gotten to know how to keep Macleod appeased, and where his weak points were, mainly filing reports and workplace organisation.

As a detective, Ross thought there was no one better, and as a colleague and friend, he still remembered Macleod helping him in the helicopter when Ross had been shot. There were times when Macleod had been turbulent, but he'd also been good. He felt during those days they had got something done. They had put away many a murderer, even prevented a few, but times were changing and so were the office dynamics.

Angus had asked him whether he wanted to become a Detective Sergeant, and Ross had answered honestly—he hadn't actually thought of it. If his current boss Hope McGrath moved up to Detective Inspector, now that Macleod had almost vacated that position for Detective Chief Inspector, he wondered if Clarissa Urquhart would just simply slot in as the Sergeant on the team. It was always funny that she and Hope held the same rank, and yet, clearly, Hope was seen as the senior.

Clarissa was rough around the edges, had a habit of calling him Als which wasn't really ideal, but her flamboyance and outright determination was a key part of the team. Still, she wasn't going to be around forever. *Retirement can't be that far away for her*, he thought.

Usually in a case, Ross was rushed off his feet, but just for five minutes, he was getting a chance to think. This was due to the distance he had to walk from the clubhouse down to the fifteenth tee. When he'd asked the green keeper where to go, he'd been pointed down the eighteenth fairway, then told to cut across. There he would find the fifteenth green with the large pond beside it, as well as the folly, and then he had to simply walk up from the green to the tee box above. Of course, the tee box would be marked off with police tape and have the various forensic officers running around it, so Ross wasn't too worried about missing it.

As he walked, the snow continued to fall, and he saw there

was a thin white dusting on the ground. It was that time of year when you just didn't know how or when the snow would come. In December, you could be reasonably sure it would lie, but at this time of year, it could be here one moment and gone the next. The north of Scotland was a funny place to live.

At this time of year, you went from cold wet days to days of glorious sunshine in the winter. Cold, crisp, and clear, those days were wonderful to be alive in and made up for standing around freezing. Other days, the rain just seemed to pelt down on you, or that misty spray pervaded your coat, reaching your bones and chilling you from inside. The Highlands had been his home all his life, and Ross loved it.

He was also experiencing a first. Never had he walked backwards down a golf course. He didn't play himself, although he went out with Angus who had shared his knowledge, so Ross had a vague idea about what was going on.

As he cleared the eighteenth hole and started to cut through for the green of the fifteenth, Ross could hear a robin, one of the distinct bird calls he could recognise. He was no ornithologist, but one thing he knew, he did enjoy listening to the birds as he walked. Trekking along the path, he looked left and right, and saw what was rather dense woodland on either side. He could understand how you could hide here; it wouldn't be that difficult. But the path he was on had stones underfoot. It was one of the more formal paths, although he did see others cutting off, pressed down grass by the mossy underside of the trees.

As he reached the path that led up from the fifteenth green to the tee box, Ross could see the forensic officers at work. He guessed he was a bit like them when he sat in front of the computer, head down, focused on going through the routines, knowing it would trawl something up. On reaching the fifteenth tee, Ross worked in an outward spiral with a pen and paper in front of him, sketching where he saw paths go off. He began to follow them, disappearing into wood and realising that many crossed up and met, or delivered you to another part of the course. However, some of them took you out towards the road, as had been mentioned by Jenny Maggert.

It was maybe only a five to ten-minute walk, and once there, the outer wall of the course seemed rather lacking. At one point, the path came down and passed through a hole in the wall, straight out to the road. Ross looked up and down the road where he noted some traffic cameras. He made a note where they were; he would check them.

Ross picked up his phone, looked at the roads around on the map on the screen. He saw there weren't that many, but he also realised that he was close to the small village of Newtonmoray. It had grown with a housing development on the side like most of the areas around Inverness, but there was an old part of a village, the place the golf club had been based on. However, the houses were probably closer to the old course than the new.

Ross turned around, came back towards the fifteenth tee and started out on another path. Between the crisscross patterns he was following, Ross realised there was a lot of land, and with the victim having been stabbed, or at least slashed with a knife, there was a possibility the knife could have been flung or hidden anywhere around here. To find such a thing would be difficult in the terrain. They could bring the dogs out, but to hand-search this would be slow and arduous. And there was nothing to suggest that the knife was out here in the first place, nothing to say the murderer hadn't taken the knife with them.

Jona had said that the knife was different, not something she'd seen, so maybe it was ornate. Maybe it meant something.

Ross picked up his mobile, called the station and got through to a constable who he tasked with collecting the footage from the traffic cameras he'd spotted. He'd return and go through it at the station, not try and work up here. It was nice to be not too far from home. He knew that if he was not working through the night, he was going home, not to a hotel. The trouble with these cases was, and especially with Macleod, he could be up all night. The boss got the bit between his teeth when he thought they were going somewhere. You were in, and you didn't walk out on Macleod. He never said you had to stay, but you never walked.'

Ross's next call was to Sergeant Halford, requesting some help from uniform in setting up some traffic stops to ask if anyone had seen anything. Not now, but the next morning, for that was the time when traffic would have been passing. Ross could see how someone could get easily up to the fifteenth tee without being seen, and, in fact, decided he needed to prove a point. He gave a call to Jona.

'Ross, this is Jona. What do you need?'

'I don't need anything. Are you up on the fifteenth? I thought I saw you.'

'Yes. Running through some things, tidying up. Why?'

'I'm not there at the moment. I'll be there shortly. I want you to look out for me. Give me a call when you spot me.'

'Okay,' said Jona. 'Bit unusual, but all right.'

Ross looked at what he was wearing. The jacket was black, the boots brown, grey charcoal trousers underneath part of his suit, and trousers that were soon to get wet because he was going to walk in and behind trees and through some quite high foliage. Yet, in a strange way, this would be fun.

He started off at the wall where the path met the road and walked in. After three or four minutes, he cut off the path and started stalking behind trees, trying to work a path back up to the fifteenth. The land rose to that tee box, and beside him was heavily wooded. When he got closer, he trailed round behind large bushes to a point where he eventually stopped and was able to look at Jona. Through the undergrowth, he could see her peering, turning this way and that, looking out for him. He tried to be careful, quietly stepping round, then realised if he went down onto his knees, he would be underneath one of the bushes, and could come out through it. He would almost be able to touch her.

Slowly, he clambered down, trying to hold his breath. He walked forward, and he heard the crack of a branch. Ross froze, but Jona didn't move. She was looking out the other side and then back to whatever it was she was working at. Somebody came up with a file, a piece of paper to sign, which she did. Then someone showed her a bag of something, and Ross continued to get closer. The only thing between Jona and him was the path. He would still have to cross the path.

Ross decided he'd try and do this in a sprint, see if he could put a hand on her before she noticed. Slowly he crept forward, wishing the wind would blow a little bit stronger, a little bit more noise through the trees, for now it was relatively calm. Snow was still falling and his nose felt cold. His hands were thankfully gloved, keeping the cold at bay as best they could, but he was down in a drain and the grass at the side of it had made his trousers soaking wet and he started to feel chills at the knees. *Well*, thought Ross, *I'm not hanging about here any longer*.

He hunched down, went forward a few steps, then suddenly leapt out of the drain onto the path, and ran over. Just as Jona turned round, Ross touched her on the shoulder.

'Hey,' she said. 'Where'd you come from?'

'Did you see me at all? Hear me?' he asked excitedly.

'No, no, not at all. Just heard footsteps on the path behind me.'

'Look over there,' he said and pointed. 'There's a drain underneath that bush. I came all the way up from the path, stepped off the path about three minutes into the trip, got up to here, close to you. You knew I was coming, and I still was able to get here and touch your shoulder before you saw me. If I'd have had a knife . . .'

'Yes,' said Jona, 'I see the point and you're not exactly built to go stealthily, are you?'

'No,' said Ross. 'I tell you what, my knees are freezing. I'm going to walk back and report this. I think you and your guys might be well employed doing a search down that path out towards the road, just in case anything dropped.'

'Thanks,' said Jona. 'With the snow coming down like this, night about to fall, the only thing I wanted to do was to be out here even longer.'

'I'll get some food and drinks for you. I've had teas and coffees going inside from the ladies that ran the restaurant in there.'

'Well, just make sure it all gets this far as well,' said Jona.

Ross gave an apologetic look, but then he turned and marched back down the path from the fifteenth to the eighteenth and up to the clubhouse. Once inside, he made a beeline to the restaurant and grabbed the head waiter he had got hold of earlier. He started asking that some soup be made

47

up, sandwiches done and left out for people here, but also that a small batch of it could be put into flasks. He quickly coordinated a constable to help with that, advising that Jona's team should be getting something soon.

Ross then made a call to see how they were getting on with the CCTV and was pleasantly surprised to find out it was on its way to be collected. He said he'd be back later that night to start going through it with someone, but they were to get on with it. Then he bumped into Hope who seemed quite flustered.

'Have you been down?' asked Hope, and then saw the wet knees.

'Yes, I've been down,' said Ross. 'You can get up from the road all the way up to the fifteenth tee quite easily. I asked Jona to look out for me, snuck up and got a hand on her before she even spotted me. And I wasn't going that stealthily. Someone who really knew what they were doing could get there easily.'

'So, you reckon Mr Mackintosh could have been attacked quickly and then they could have got back out without ever being seen?'

'Yes,' said Ross. 'The strange thing was setting him up like a puppet, standing there over a shot. That seems a little odd. Why not just get up, stab, stab, kill, back out. The idea of him being positioned like a mannequin, there's something in that,' said Ross. 'There's a connection there of some sort.'

'I think you're right,' said Hope, 'but we'll get that from the background of the people, which I believe you need to be on as well.'

'Of course,' said Ross. 'In case you need it, soup and sandwiches are coming from the restaurant. I'd try and eat something now if I was you, Hope. Macleod never did that.

Macleod went on an empty stomach when he was running these things. I always kept bringing it up with him.

'Something wrong with being my waiter?' asked Hope.

'Nothing,' said Ross, 'nothing at all. Don't need to take it that way. I was just saying about Seoras.'

Ross didn't know quite what to do then. Should he walk off? Then she would think he was offended. If he stayed, what was the next awkward piece of information?

He looked out of the window, saw a police car, and then a figure getting out of it. There was a long coat and a hat, and then a burgundy scarf. The burgundy scarf was new but had been bought by Jane, Macleod's partner, three weeks previous. She must've dressed him this morning, told him if he was on tele, he had to look the part. Ross gave a chuckle, then turned to Hope.

'Cavalry's here,' he said. 'I'll let him know where the soup and sandwiches are.' He almost ran from the room. She laughed at him, telling him to get out.

Chapter 06

Macleod stepped out of the police car and took a moment to look around. His long coat wasn't keeping out the cold that well, but he seemed to feel it much more these days. The long burgundy scarf flopped down about his front, and he gathered one end of it, throwing it around his neck. As he looked across, he saw a TV camera pointing at him as he did this. *Oh well,* he thought, *police dress disasters must be a new programme,* but he gave the cameraman a scowl, so that he knew he was the only one happy about it.

Macleod went through the police lines, getting his usual nod from constables aware of who he was, and then passed Ross going the other way.

'Evening, sir,' said Ross, almost cheerfully.

'What's happening?' asked Macleod.

'That's really up to the sergeant to brief for that, sir,' said Ross. 'I could tell you but she's the hub of the information.'

He is right, thought Macleod. *I'm the DCI now. I need to go and talk to the investigating officer. Hope's got the scene. I should go to Hope. It's not my team anymore, is it? Oh, it is.*

He wasn't sure of the dynamics anymore. He wasn't sure how this worked. The DCI never thought that Macleod's team were his, but then some of the former DCIs hadn't been that good. He needed to be here, he felt. Needed to advise, needed to make sure things were going in the right direction, but he didn't want to take over either. He gave Ross a curt nod and turned towards the clubhouse.

As he got closer, he asked a constable whether he had seen Sergeant McGrath, and he was told to go up a flight of stairs where she was running things in the makeshift incident room. Macleod shook a thin line of snow off his shoes as he entered, and then traipsed up the stairs before finding Hope in a large room sitting down at a desk.

She was talking to several constables and so Macleod entered quietly. As he did so, a couple of the constables snapped up, almost to attention, not because they had to but more because they realised who had entered the room. Macleod waved a hand to them, almost dismissively, and then walked over to an unused table in the far corner. He saw Hope rise but shouted across the room to her that it would wait until she finished what she was at.

As he sat watching, he scanned the room. *Might not be quite as I would set it up, but then again, most of these rooms were set up by Ross or Hope previously for me.* Macleod had heard word of a news conference and wanted to get everybody off on a correct foot. Maybe that's what he would do. Take the news conferences—let Hope get on with it.

It was an awkward situation because he was the acting DCI, yet still a DI, still technically in charge of the team but there was no way he could run things that way at the moment. He'd be off his feet, backwards and forwards. He needed to be a DCI, he needed Hope to act like the DI, and Clarissa to fill in as their Sergeant. He was aware though that Ross would then

51

find himself alone at the bottom of the chain. They were short of staff, and more people would be required.

Somebody new would be necessary. *Had Clarissa given thought to being the sergeant, being the one running the team for Hope? Would she want that? Did it make sense?* He knew Clarissa was a good officer, but she was not someone to be running a team. The Rottweiler, they called her. Well, that's what she was, could sink her teeth into anything, could hound people until the truth came out, but what she wasn't, was a people manager.

Macleod pondered this as a cup of coffee came his way. He looked around to see if Ross had organised it. Then he saw Hope staring across at him. About five minutes later, she marched over, giving him a brief smile but he could tell she was obviously under pressure.

'How's it going then?'

'Fine, have you heard any different?'

'No,' said Macleod. 'I'm just asking. I've been out of the loop. I've been tied up all day with those two . . .' He wanted to say clowns. He wanted to say waste of time but he didn't. He was the DCI now; he had to set an example. 'Visitors,' he said quickly.

'Visitors,' said Hope. 'We are learning new words.' He gave a wry smile.

'Anyway, enough of that; what's happening? Are you on top of it?'

'Of course, I'm on top of it; just a lot to get on with.'

'I didn't mean that,' said Macleod. 'I don't mean the procedures; I mean the case. Do you have any ideas yet?'

'No,' said Hope. 'Sandy Mackenzie, killed on the fifteenth hole, Club Secretary. There are two courses here. Old one, new one. The new one might be getting a visit from the tour—the golf tour that is, lots of money, lots of publicity. Old one's going to get left behind. The board is mixed between the two; lot of friction about it.'

'Okay,' said Macleod quietly. 'What's your move at the moment?'

'Searching the scene; see if we can find the murder weapon. Jona says the man was stabbed but it's a different sort of blade. We've also been checking how you could get to the fifteenth tee box without being seen on a golf course where the holes are incredibly open, though the undergrowth is not. Mackintosh was put up like a mannequin, complete with his golf club, and on a hole called Sandy's Folly. There may be a deliberate connection because the hole seems to have been a jibe at him.

'I've got the board coming in because I want to speak to them directly. They would be potential suspects. Apparently, the man was well liked. He was a golfer through and through, been at this club for a long time, and while he had differences of opinion with people, most people say that they liked him. The other thing is that the main issue with the tour coming seems to be well contained in that it was only being openly fought out at board level. Others have heard about it though, the ground staff in particular.'

'People on the ground always know about it,' said Macleod. 'It's very difficult to keep things quiet. You're going to need a press conference at some point. Do you want me to cover that off?'

'Well, I'm better at press conferences. You know that,' said Hope.

'Yes, but . . .'

'But what?' asked Hope. 'I'll do it.'

53

'You're going to run short,' said Macleod. 'You personally are going to run short.'

'What do you mean? You don't think I'm up to this.'

'I think you're more than up to it but you're going to run short. Look, when I did this, you took the press off me so I could do what I was good at. The press is just another thing; any of us could do it. Some of us do it better than others but it's not what's going to solve the case. What's going to solve the case is you, and you thinking through the details and you chasing things down. If you're stuck with a press, you can't do that, Hope. That's why I never did the press stuff. It's rubbish—it's just a junket. It's just something you have to go and do; it is not part and parcel of getting to the bottom of a case. Unless your boss makes you do it, get out of it if you can.'

Hope stared at Macleod. 'What's with the scarf?'

'Cutting an image,' said Macleod. 'Jane said I needed to cut an image. I need to look like a DCI, not like this hop-along inspector. She said I made the scruffs of the street look impressive at times with what I wore. I need to look good for the TV now, as a DCI. She said I was always outshone by predecessors.'

'Yes, but you weren't corrupt like some of them,' said Hope. 'But seriously, Seoras, let me run this. Let me run it the way I want.'

'Okay,' said Macleod, 'but you need to keep me closely informed. If I didn't think you could do this, I'd have a DI coming in to help,' he said. 'So, don't think I'm not trusting you, but we have got to get this right. If we don't get this right, it could harm you. It's not fair. It's like you're doing a job interview with this case. That's not fair, but that's the way they'll see it. At the moment, they think you'll be great, smiling Hope, good-looking, six-feet Hope. Hope with the red hair. Hope that sends a good image about the department instead of the old fart that went before her.'

Macleod thought that she would laugh at this, but instead, she looked incredulous.

'Six-feet, red hair. Who cares? I get results.'

'No,' said Macleod. 'Not in their world. In their world, you don't get results. In their world, I got the results. Now, when I did and it came from you, or it came from Ross, or it came from Clarissa, I always, *always*, held up what you did. I always held you up, but they don't look at it like that. 'Who's running the team? Oh, it's Macleod? That's Macleod's case. Macleod did this. Macleod did that.' Utter nonsense!

'That's how it works. This time, Macleod's up above. He's got Hope running it; therefore, it'll be on Hope. It won't reflect on Ross, it won't reflect on Clarissa, and they won't care that you're shorthanded. So, keep me informed closely.'

'You have got to let me have free rein though, Seoras. You can't control me with this. I'm not just running around in the way we were before.'

'No, but you're also not the DI yet. That is the problem, Hope. It'll be a test run for you. They'll be assessing you for DI, but if it goes wrong, it still reflects on me because I should have been there covering off. We've always been good together. Keep it that way. I'll come in with the board. Are they here yet?'

'Not yet,' she said, 'although . . .' She walked over to the window. 'That looks like some of them now. Alastair Begley is already here somewhere. He's the operating officer, but I think we get them all in together.'

'If that's how you want to play it.'

'That's how I want to play it,' said Hope. 'I want to lay down some ground rules to them and I want them to tell me what's going on in front of each other.'

'Sensible,' said Macleod. 'Forces a reaction. Watch the other faces. See who blinks.'

'Glad you approve,' said Hope.

Macleod let it slide. 'I'll let you get on,' he said. 'As soon as you're ready with the board, give us a shout. Not sure where I'll be.'

'There's soup and sandwiches downstairs,' said Ross from across the room.

'I'll be downstairs, then,' said Macleod.

He walked out of the room but stopped before going down the stairs to look back inside. Hope was talking to others, and he loved how she commanded the room. It did help, her size, the shocking red hair. She was certainly more approachable than he, but he knew she'd have to be tough stepping up. *She was ready, though, wasn't she?* he asked himself. He was bothered, though, and there was no resounding answer.

Macleod walked downstairs and followed his nose until he walked into a large room where a canteen of soup was positioned on the side. He watched several constables pouring some into flasks. On his arrival, they turned suddenly.

'Would you like some, sir?'

'Seoras,' he said quietly.

'Would you like some, Seoras, sir?' said the young lad.

'You're giving me soup. There's no need to be nervous with it.' Then Macleod recognised who the young man was. He had got a hold of Macleod in one of the most recent cases when they said Macleod wasn't finding a child killer, and this man had throttled Macleod as he'd looked to release a suspect out of the front door of the station.'

'All said and done,' said Macleod. 'No need for sir, just Seoras. I'll take a soup and a sandwich, please, when you get a minute. But if that's for the guys outside, get that done first.'

Macleod watched them hurry, almost splashing the soup and took a place up at a table in the far corner of the room. He watched a man come in, have a discussion with the head waiter, and then look to go out again. Macleod called over to him.

'Excuse me,' he said. The man turned and frowned at him. 'Excuse me, could you come and sit a moment?' asked Macleod.

The man marched over. 'If you don't mind, I'm quite busy. There's a lot to do.'

'There's always a lot to do,' said Macleod. 'Sit down, please. You must be one of the board members. Possibly the operations person.'

'Are you press?' asked the man.

'No,' said Macleod, reaching inside his coat and pulling out his warrant card. 'Acting DCI Macleod. You've probably spoken already to DS McGrath. I'll be joining her to meet the board. I was just wondering how far away we are from all gathering?'

'Alastair Begley. They should be here within the next twenty minutes,' the man said.

'Good,' said Macleod. 'Looking for a spot of soup. Suggest getting some yourself. It could be a long night.'

'I'm finding that,' said the man. 'How long will you be here, anyway?' He seemed quite testy, but there had been a murder at the end of the day. 'And will we be able to open up the old course, get at least one course open for the members?'

'I don't think that's wise at the moment. We're in the first day of having somebody killed on a tee box. Who's killed Mr. Mackintosh? Is it a random killer? Will he be going around the golf course killing people? Is it something to do specifically with Mr Mackintosh? Is it to do with the old and the new course and the issues between?' Macleod saw the eyebrows jump at that point. 'Sergeant McGrath will advise you when you can open again, and what you can open. If you feel the need for the members to be back, then please, see her.'

The man nodded. As he went to turn away, Macleod gave a cough.

'How well did you know Mr. Mackintosh?'

'Sandy. Very well, on the board with me. A finer man you'll never meet.'

'It's always interesting,' said Macleod. 'People always talk about how good someone is after they're dead.'

'Are you accusing me of something?'

'No,' said Macleod. 'I just find that, in general, don't you? Wonderful things are always said about people after they die, but it's the things that are said before that really tell you what people think.'

The man looked at Macleod, teeth gritted, before turning and walking off. *He looked genuinely offended*, thought Macleod. *Probably not him.*

Chapter 07

Hope and Macleod walked together into the boardroom to see the large wooden table around which seven seats were positioned. One was empty, that of Sandy Mackintosh. Macleod wondered if either of them should sit there. The other board members had already come in and taken their positions. No one having provided extra seats for the two police officers, Macleod leaned into Hope. 'Do you want to do this standing?' he whispered.

'There's a seat there for you if you want it,' she said.

'I'm not sitting down in a dead person's seat,' he said. 'I just thought we should get the seats now rather than look like we're half-knackered in ten minutes.'

'Well, I'm good to stand. Besides,' she said, 'I'm six feet; these guys sitting down, I dwarf them.'

Macleod gave a smile and relocated himself to the corner of the room, slouching on the wall, offering the floor to Hope.

'Thank you for coming in today. I'm sorry about what has happened. I regret to inform you that Sandy Mackintosh, your colleague, was murdered on the fifteenth tee this morning. As such, the course is closed, and we are investigating. I need to build up a picture of the place, of you as a board who worked with him, and of Sandy's life outside of the club. I'd be appreciative of your candour and frankness. Can I start by asking for a brief history of this club and for your names? Just for the record and for the DCI.'

'Maybe I can do that,' said a rather big-shouldered man. He had large jowls as well and seemed quite forceful. 'I'm Andrew Peters, the Club Chairman and I think I can speak for all of us in saying that Sandy Mackintosh will be missed. Sandy was at this club for a long time. Also, a friend of mine, we used to eat dinner with our wives here every Saturday night for many years. It feels like a part of me has disappeared today.

'Beside me here is Deputy Chairman Cecil Ayers. Cecil's been around the club for a good while now, too. Alastair Begley, you've probably met, our Chief Operating Officer. Orla Smith over there is our staff manager, and beside her is the Golf Operations Manager, Pádraig O'Reilly. The newest member of the board, however, is Amy Johnson and probably a good deal younger than the rest of us as well.'

Andrew Peters flashed a smile at her sitting in a crisp black outfit, a neatly tied ponytail, and some rather expensive-looking glasses.

'Do continue,' said Hope.

'Well,' said Mr Peters, 'this golf club is over one hundred years old. We were formed initially as a links golf club with the old course which is well respected but has never really truly achieved its full potential. Unfortunately, these days links golf is not held in the esteem that it used to be; people want more American courses. Our new course was built less than ten years ago. It's only coming to fruition now and hopefully, soon we'll be having a tour-level event here. Those negotiations are underway.'

'If I may,' said Amy Johnson, 'golf clubs these days are in trouble, Sergeant, and because of that, we need to acquire more revenue. If you operate a course that has been used as part of a tour, has held any significant events like the Ryder Cup or one of the majors, you can attract high-value clientele. Unfortunately, the Open is not open to us because they play it on a links course. Our links course was never going to be able to achieve that distinction.'

'You don't know that,' said Pádraig O'Reilly. 'You don't know that. That course with the right investment, that could be as good as any of them. St Andrews couldn't hold a light to that course.'

'You're right there,' said Alastair Begley.

'Nonsense,' said Andrew Peters, his large frame now sitting on his elbows at the desk. Hope could see the drool at the side of his mouth as he spoke, which reminded her of a bulldog, and not the lovable kind.

'Well, it's not golf, is it?' said Cecil Ayers, the Deputy Chairman. 'It's not real golf. At the end of the day, what's important is the tradition. How we keep golf. Golf shouldn't become some sort of mass-marketing thing. What are we going to have, shootouts? Maybe we can all start together. Maybe we could play the odd hole with a windmill in the middle.'

'There's no need to be facetious,' said Peters.

'If I may, gentlemen,' said Amy Johnson, and Hope noticed how most of them looked to her. There was more than just simply respect there. She thought that a couple of them looked at her as if she was a great addition for the mantlepiece, something good to look at. 'The needs of the club and the needs of making money required that we went with a new course.'

'Money,' said the other woman at the table. She was older, maybe in her early forties, Hope thought, and Orla Smith now stood up to speak. 'I'm not a golfer. I've never been a golfer, but from what I understand from those of you who are, we don't want to turn this into Blackpool.

'What sort of a comment is that?' thundered Andrew Peters.

Pádraig O'Reilly stood up, jumping to Orla's defence. 'We don't want to be tacky town. They don't call it the Blackpool Golf Course, do they? They call it Lytham & St Annes because it's not Blackpool—it's not tat. It's not there for the kind of people who watch all that nonsense on TV. Next, you'll be telling us we should have a reality show about how we got this damn course ready.'

'That was an option they outlined before,' said Amy Johnson.

'Whoa,' said Hope suddenly, 'we're all getting a little heated here. Can we all sit down for a start? I prefer it if only I and the DCI were the ones standing.'

Hope watched Pádraig O'Reilly adjust Orla's seat and let her sit down before he sat down himself. She noted that Alastair Begley had his head in his hands. 'I'd like to know more about this tour-level event. Could you explain that to me, Mr Chairman?'

'Of course,' said Peters. 'Basically, the tour wants to come to different parts of Scotland. Scotland was mainly links courses, but they do want to be able to show something different. We've built a course that could even one day bring the Ryder Cup to Scotland.'

'Bollocks,' said O'Reilly.

'In a minute, Mr O'Reilly,' said Hope, 'this won't work unless I'm listening to one person. I'd like to hear your opinion in a minute. Please continue, Mr Peters.'

'Well,' said Peters, 'the tour wants a more modern course. They want the entire course set up for how the cameras will look at it. The old course out there, it doesn't look that great. When you see it on TV, everything flattens so the contours don't look—well, a lot of the links courses, frankly, look rather dull. The more modern ones, you can have a nice flower bed behind the action. You can have large drops, a bit of waterfall going on, water here and there. They really look quite spectacular.'

'They're not real courses. We don't make courses for the bloody TV people.'

'Mr O'Reilly,' said Hope, 'enough. I'll come to you in a minute. I mean that.' As if to enforce her point, Hope stepped over and O'Reilly suddenly was looking up at a woman that dwarfed him. 'What are the chances of getting this course as a tour event?' asked Hope.

'Frankly, if I may, Mr Chairman,' said Amy Johnson, 'very good. We've worked hard. We're almost there, and in truth, within the next couple of weeks, I think the deal will be done.'

'How can the deal be done?' raged Alastair Begley. 'Explain to me how the deal can be done.'

'Indeed,' said Hope. 'My colleague was talking to the ground staff, and they have an opinion that to run here as a board, you operate on the principle of dormie five. As I understand it, five out of seven of you must give the go-ahead for anything to happen. Clearly, Mr Peters, you and Miss Johnson support this measure. I'm not sure how the rest of you sit apart from Mr O'Reilly and Mr Begley. That, to me, says there's two on one side and two on the other. What about you, Mr Ayres?'

The Deputy Chairman looked up. 'It's not right,' he said,

'we need to keep the traditions. This would bring attention to the club, but in the wrong way. We'll get rabble coming in and there'll be a pay-to-play course, not a membership, not what makes us what we are. Golf is about more than just what happens out on the course. It's a family. Sandy understood that. Sandy really understood that.'

The room went silent for a moment and Hope could feel the respect that some of these people had for Mackintosh.

'What about you? Is it Mrs Smith or Miss Smith?'

'You can call me Orla,' said Orla Smith standing up.

'You don't have to stand up to speak,' said Hope, 'you can sit at the table; it's fine.'

'Oh, sorry. I'm a staff manager. I organise the people. I'm not a golfer. I understand what Cecil says about this being a club. When we employ staff, we try to do that. You try to have a community in here, the restaurant, everything else we've got going. I helped build that over these last lot of years, and now, we're talking about having a restaurant for people who come once in a blue moon. You become a commodity. I'm not sure I like that.'

Hope noticed that Pádraig O'Reilly was smiling broadly at the woman. 'And what's the big objection, Mr O'Reilly?' asked Hope. 'You clearly are against it.'

'Absolutely. Things have been forced through. We got the new course put in, but it wasn't going to be the size it is. We're spending money on getting it ready. We're going to spend a lot more. Cecil voted through the money to get the new course a proper chance, but he's not up with putting the TV in. He's not up with changing it.'

'If we're going to have a parkland course, it needed to be done well,' said Cecil; 'that's why I went with that. This is a

64

step too far.'

'That's how Sandy saw it as well,' said Alastair. 'Some of us understood that the new course was not an evil thing but that some members like that type of golf, or the choice of both. Not everyone likes links and that's fine. But we run as one club. Now we've become a marketing exercise. Tour events are not always that great. You have to prep. You can't play the course for a long time before. You've got to get it ready. They all come in, the media circus, then they all pile out leaving the mess. This is our club; it's not a company.'

'And things are not decided,' said Pádraig O'Reilly. 'Mr Chairman sits there speaking as if this is all done and dusted. It's not. It's not voted through. We still haven't got the full details put on the table. He knows them; she knows them.'

Pádraig O'Reilly was pointing to Amy Johnson. He maintained a cautious smile. 'Everybody else doesn't know them. We don't know what the money is and what's happening, and besides that, we're not doing it. Sandy was against it wholeheartedly.'

'So, as things stand, you have two people for it and I count four against,' said Hope. 'Do you still need five then with a seat vacant?'

'No,' said Alastair Begley, 'you need five out of seven. There must be seven to vote.'

'And he'll get some lackey in,' said O'Reilly, standing and pointing at the chairman. 'He'll get some bloody lackey of his in. Somebody who doesn't know diddly-squat about this damn club, you watch. You watch and see the manoeuvres that go on now.'

Andrew Peters stood up and Hope wondered if he was about to spring onto the table and jump along like a bulldog attacking

O'Reilly. 'How dare you. I've been at this club longer than you.'

'Yes, but you brought her in, the fancy bit of tart. Look at her. All she's about is the damn money.'

'Excuse me,' said Macleod from the corner. 'No, I'm not having that. You may not like each other, but now all I'm getting is people mouthing off insults to each other. Kindly behave.'

Hope shot a glance over at Macleod. He had said it incredibly quietly, forcing them to listen, forcing them to drop their voices. It was a masterstroke from a man, who, in her position would've quieted them by slamming his fist on the table and telling them what for, but she could see that the tension was still there although the voices had gone quieter. *It was time to change approach*, thought Hope.

'I need to know where you all were this morning, if I may. Mr Peters?'

'I was home most of the morning. I'm retired. I don't actually work anymore.'

'Can anybody confirm you were there?'

'I live alone. My wife died a few months ago. Still getting used to that.'

'Mr Ayres?'

'I'm similar,' said Cecil. 'Gives you time to devote to the club. Been retired ten years now, just at home. I don't get up too early.'

'I don't start until later,' said Orla. 'I tend to work an eleven-to-five day. I have things to care to in the morning.'

'Family and kids,' said Pádraig, 'back there this morning.'

'I was late in this morning,' said Alastair Begley, 'I was here late last night; that's the only reason. The wife was out at work, and I was in the house on my own.'

'What about you, Miss Johnson?' asked Hope.

'Well, I get up in the mornings and I was at the gym. There were plenty of people watching me this morning. I like to work out down at the gym, take a nice shower, and then a swim,' she said. 'Sets you up for the day.'

'Walking around like a strutting peacock, more like,' said O'Reilly under his breath. Hope saw Macleod's face, but she jumped in ahead of him.

'That's enough, Mr O'Reilly. I'm not here to see how good an insult you can throw at each other, though clearly, you know how to do that. I want to advise you all that we'll now step aside and interview you individually. I will be checking up on your alibis, or the lack of them. The club is going to be shut for at least two days and I want numbers from you all where I can contact you at short notice, please.'

Outside, a noise was building, and Hope moved round to look out of the window. Down below, the press were seemingly getting agitated. They'd been out there a long time and so far, they hadn't had a statement, and with the arrival of Macleod, they obviously believed they were entitled to one sooner rather than later.

'That's the press outside,' Hope said to Seoras. 'Seems like they're kicking off.'

'Light's going to go soon. They want to know if they're coming in here or we're going to do it out there.'

'Well, we can clear one of the long rooms, bring them in, sit them down,' said Andrew Peters.

'No,' said Macleod, 'I'll do it. It'll be outside and take five minutes. You'll all stay in here with Sergeant McGrath. If you don't require me, Sergeant, I'll go and sort out this press before I come back to see if you need any further assistance.'

'I've got it,' she said. 'Thank you.'

Macleod gave her a nod as he walked out, and Hope turned, staring at the faces in front of her. She was under no illusions about what Macleod had said earlier. She had hoped that of the six in front of her, they might have been able to eliminate a few. On first glance, Amy Johnson was the only one with an alibi, but she needed to dig deeper. The major debate was the issue dividing the two courses. Is that what this was about? Because if it was, Hope believed it couldn't end here, because frankly, the numbers just didn't sit.

Chapter 08

Hope McGrath picked up the phone and dialled a number that she'd got to know well. It was the mobile number for John, her partner, who was down at a conference far away. She heard it ring and ring, and eventually, a voice came on at the other end. In the background there was noise and music, and she could barely make John out as he said hello.

'How are you?' he said. She reckoned he'd had a few drinks.

'Busy. Case has broken since you've been away,' she said. 'I was just ringing to tell you I might not be able to speak much over the next couple of days.'

'Okay,' he said. 'It's going well down here.'

'It sounds it. Have you had a bit?'

He started to laugh. 'More than a bit. Been a really good conference though. Just having some drinks tonight, back in again tomorrow, and then hopefully up the road after that. I've been telling them all about you. Some of them down here even know you. Mainly the Scottish ones though. Seen you on the TV. One guy was really impressed. He said, are you . . .' John suddenly stopped. 'Actually, that was a bit rude,' he said, 'the way he put it. I said to him, she's my partner, yes.' Hope nearly laughed.

'I hope you're not down there bragging,' she said.

'Bragging? Darn right I'm bragging. Telling them all about my Hope.'

You're drunk, she thought. *You're absolutely stonking. Gone.*

'Are you okay?' asked John.

'I'm fine. Just busy,' said Hope. There was silence on the other end.

'Really?'

The question struck at Hope. 'Yes, I'm fine,' she said. 'You enjoy your conference.'

'I'm not that drunk,' he said. 'Do you want to talk about it?'

'How?' asked Hope. 'You've got stuff to do. You're in the middle of a pub by the sounds of it. No, no, no.'

'I'll walk out if you want to talk about it,' said John.

'I haven't time at the moment. We're about to brief the team. I just wanted to phone and tell you I might not be able to speak to you that often. I'll talk to you about it when you come home.'

'Okay,' said John. 'I'm looking forward to that.'

'Me too,' said Hope. 'Me too.'

She closed the call down. It was true. Having John at home was always a help. She could go home in the evening, she'd chat things through, or she could just be held. Sometimes you didn't need to talk. Sometimes you just needed a friendly face, an arm around you. She felt safe in John's arms.

It was ridiculous. If there was any threat of violence, she was the one who could handle it, not him. She was the police officer. She was the one who could figure people out. He just rented cars, and yet she felt safe in his hands. Safe when wrapped up by him. Some things were just crazy.

Ross burst into the room and then stopped, seeing Hope's

face.

'You okay? Did you want a minute? I didn't barge in, did I?'

'No, come in. We need to get this done. Where's the rest of the gang?'

'Jona is on her way. Clarissa will be here shortly. I think the boss is outside finishing up with the last of the media, and then we'll be good to go.' She watched Ross look around and then desperately run out of the room before coming back with a fresh flask of coffee.

'Everybody's getting tired,' said Ross. 'We need the coffee. Are there any more of those sandwiches?' *He was like a mother hen*, thought Hope. She didn't need a mother hen. Macleod might have. Macleod might have not thought of all these other things, because he was always so damn focused on the main issue, but Hope did. Hope was able to cover off the extras.

It was only a few minutes later when the rest of the team entered the room before Macleod joined them last. Hope was standing at the far end of the room with a table in front of her with her notes. Clarissa had sat down opposite her, Ross just to the side, and Jona sat on a table close by. Hope watched as Macleod entered the room, and stepped over to the side where Ross was.

'Sorry I'm late. A few of the media boys had to have a few things explained. They're looking to pass on vicious rumours of the golf course murderer. Told them I didn't want anything too dramatic. Probably a domestic dispute.'

'Okay,' said Hope. 'Well, coming to the close of day one, I'll probably be here for most of the night. Today I've interviewed the board and frankly, we're struggling to eliminate any of them. Only one, Amy Johnson, the Publicity and Promotions director, has any alibi for the time when Sandy Mackintosh died. I see the whole board apart from her still as potential suspects, although we haven't really put any strong links together. How are we doing on their backgrounds, Ross?'

'Still working on the dossiers,' he said. 'Should have it ready to go for tomorrow.'

'Well, tomorrow we'll be interviewing. I want you in on that with me, Clarissa.'

Clarissa looked over at Macleod who simply gave a nod. Hope turned to Ross. 'You need to keep going on the backgrounds and CCTV. The usual stuff you pick up, everything in and around, please, Alan.'

He turned to look at Macleod who held up his hand.

'Woah,' he said. 'Hope is running this investigation. Stop looking at me to give a nod to what she says. Detective Sergeant McGrath is more than capable of running this investigation, and more than that, I've put my trust in her to do it. I'm having to pick up the DCI function. Make no doubt about it, I'm still the boss, but Hope will report to me directly and will talk to me about the case directly. She will be running it. I'm here to assist, because we are a person short at the moment until we can sort out everyone's new designations within the station. I'll be helping with interviews. I'll be helping out with any spadework I can outside of my other function. As for both of you, Hope is the one who will tell you what to do, how she wants it done, and I expect, as ever, you to do as instructed, get it done well and challenge if you think something is wrong, but you challenge Hope, not me, and you don't look to me for confirmation. Are we understood?'

'Yes, sir,' said Ross, and put his head down.

'Got it,' said Clarissa and turned to look at Hope. 'Sorry.'

Hope wasn't quite sure how to feel, but at least Seoras had clarified it for everyone else.

'The obvious motive here is that Sandy Mackintosh was against the new course, and more than that, what the new course represented, a change away from being a golf club into being a more of a money-making machine. He had friends on the board that agreed with him, but yet the new course and everything else had been pushed this far. I'm told that the tour is at the point of making an offer to actually come and be hosted here at the new course. Amy Johnson, the Publicity and Promotions Director, and the Club Chairman, Andrew Peters, seem to be thick on this. Everybody else seems to be against. As I understand it, they operate a policy called dormie five here, a policy that states that they need five of the board members to agree out of seven before they can move proposals forward.

'That's correct,' said Ross. 'I've gone into the constitution and legally they have to obtain that.'

'Good. We've definitely got a potential motive with this.'

'We have,' said Clarissa, 'but forgive me. Taking out Sandy Mackintosh leaves two to four. Can they vote on that?'

'No,' said Ross. 'There needs to be seven. There must be seven. Again, that's in the constitution. They'll be holding elections very quickly if they need to get a decision.'

'Quickly?' queried Hope.

'Absolutely,' said Ross. 'They need to get a stand-in secretary at least. Normally what they'd do is hold an election. Somebody comes in and unless they have any good reason to throw them out within the first year, they stay and they get re-elected every two years in the post. Some of the posts are obviously highly paid. The Publicity and Promotions Director, that post, as I understand it, is part of an interview process. The board then recommends and everybody in the club ratifies.'

'Okay,' said Hope. 'So, they're going to vote on the vacant position. If we get somebody in there who's for changing the club and having a more money-orientated view, that will give us a reason for bumping Sandy Mackintosh out of the way.'

'That would only give us three to four,' said Clarissa. 'That won't work. They've got to get a five to two. That means they've got to bump off another two people. That means . . .'

'If that's the motive, they've got to work around it.'

'Forgive me,' said Jona. 'I'm obviously here because I deal with what's been left behind, but if you start doing that, won't the tour get a little bit worried that they're now going to be promoting their event at the club where everybody died, especially if somebody's going to stick them up on a tee in this macabre fashion. It would be much more sensible to try and kill them off in what looked like accidents.'

'That's true,' said Hope. 'That's very true, but what other right reasons have we got? I mean, they do know each other.'

'They do,' said Macleod. 'There were a lot of passions running earlier on in that boardroom. I think some of these people know each other better out of the boardroom than in it.'

'Are you thinking Amy Johnson then?' asked Hope. 'You think that's how she got that position?'

'I don't think she slept her way to that position,' said Macleod. 'That's not what I'm suggesting. She's too much of an operator to have to sleep with people. I think she could push and pull people this way and that and muscle her way in without needing to actually go to bed with them.'

'But you think there's other things going on?'

'It's just a hunch from the outside,' said Macleod. 'I don't want to cloud anybody's vision yet. You're going to interview them. Let's see what they bring up.'

'How are you getting on, Jona?' asked Hope.

'Working on what sort of a blade did this. I've needed to go and outsource so it's going to take a little bit longer. We've got to get photographs of the wound off tonight to colleagues outside Inverness. We are also searching through the undergrowth though we're not doing that tonight. We've put a couple of people out there to protect the scene and the area around the scene. We'll get it searched tomorrow. No idea if the weapon's there, but from Ross's walk earlier on, it seems a possibility we should check.'

'You definitely could come up from that road,' said Ross. 'We'll get through the CCTVs, see if any cars were about. It might not give us definitive proof, but if we can find somebody in that area, if we can identify any potential suspects who were in the area at the time, that would give opportunity. Then we can maybe look at how they did it, why they did it.'

'I'll need to talk to the tour as well,' said Hope, 'bring them in.'

'They won't simply come into the club. They can't do that,' said Macleod. 'You're talking about potentially putting a tour here. They're now walking into the middle of a murder investigation. They won't want to associate with that and need to protect their brand. We'll have press out there tomorrow and then we'll be interviewing the tour. That means they'll put two and two together to get nine; murder involves the tour somehow. You know what the press are like—they'll concoct some story. They'll put a link in. We'll need to meet the tour somewhere else.'

'Well, I'll go and meet them somewhere else.'

'You've got your interviews tomorrow,' said Macleod. 'Let me take it. Without being daft, the tour will prefer that. DCI Macleod comes to talk. It's showing a higher level and it's not accusatory. You're running this investigation. I'm just having a chat. I know I said I'd try and keep out of the way, but in this case, I think it makes sense that I go and talk. Let's you get down to the nitty-gritty of your suspects.'

Hope felt a little bit deflated as if Macleod was starting to tell her what to do.

'It makes sense,' said Clarissa. 'Seoras is right. It's not a good situation we're in. We could do with having our structures in place, but they're not there, and this makes sense. Besides, gets him out of our hair, doesn't it?' Hope looked at Clarissa's face, which was smiling, but she was very definite about what she was saying.

'I agree,' said Ross. Hope flicked her head over to look at him. 'Oh, sorry,' he said. 'Was my opinion not wanted?'

'Always, Alan. It's always wanted,' she said. 'To sum up after a day, we don't really have a motive. We need to know more about what's behind the man; see who Sandy Mackintosh really was. We also need to see who all the board are. We need to identify what knife was used, see if that ties to anyone, and we're looking for the public to give us some idea of who was in the area. We don't have a lot,' said Hope, and she felt somewhat deflated.

'No, we don't,' said Macleod, 'but we never do. I never had a lot after the first day. Usually a load of questions, nothing else, but I had you guys,' said Macleod.

'And you've got us,' said Clarissa.

Hope nodded, then advised them all that she'd be working

out of here for tonight and watched as they left the room to go and do whatever tasks they needed. Macleod hung back and waited until the door was closed.

'You good?' he asked.

'Of course, I'm good.'

'I'm not asking as your DCI, Hope. I'm asking as your friend.'

She gave him a weak smile and he walked across to her. 'Why do I feel like I'm on trial? Why am I on trial after all this time of working with you? Why don't they just trust you? Why don't they just . . .'

Macleod put his hand on her shoulder. 'I know you. I know how you work. I know what you're good at. I know where you can improve, but I also know what you've got around you. You'll get this. Trust yourself, trust the team. DI can be a lonely place, but you're never alone. You need to understand that, and if you ever need to talk about it, you can always talk to Seoras. It doesn't have to be the DCI.'

Hope put her hand up on Macleod's shoulder and they stood in front of each other looking like two bowling pins supporting each other lest they fall over.

'Thanks, Seoras, but we do look a little bit ridiculous.'

'Well, I didn't know if you'd find a hug patronising,' he said.

Hope reached forward and hugged him and then stepped back. 'Thank you.' Macleod simply nodded before walking away. 'You're going to be about?' she asked.

'Not unless you need me. DCI. I go to bed at night.'

'You're still the DI though as well.'

'Not at this time of night,' he said.

'Love to Jane then,' said Hope. As she watched him go, she thought about what Macleod would do at this point. Was there paperwork to look through? Yes. Did she need to check off a few lists? Probably, but he would've sat down and thought about what he learned. He would've sat and mulled things over. She was the centre of this investigation. She was the one having to send the troops out to do the work. She stood and watched Macleod get into a police car and be driven away from the golf club. The place was fairly silent now, and she sat down with a cup of coffee and put her feet up on the desk.

'Come on, Hope,' she said. 'What's going on?'

Chapter 09

Macleod was feeling somewhat unsettled in his new role. There seemed to be more paperwork these days. There seemed to be more meetings with other departments. There seemed to be less time spent out chasing down the bad guys, and at the moment, he had only just moved up to cover the DCI position. He wasn't yet the permanent fixture.

When he was able to take a meeting with Dermot McKinley from the European tour in an Inverness hotel at ten o'clock the following morning, he was actually feeling pretty chuffed. He would get out of the office; no one could bother him. Well, no one unless it was truly important.

He might field a call from Hope, Ross, or even Clarissa, or maybe even some of the other sergeants or members of the force he fed intelligence information into, but what he wouldn't do was get stuck in some sort of finances meeting or work schedule. Macleod was very clear about what you did. You worked until you caught them. Yes, you might go home after a couple of days because the trail was cold at that point, but the job didn't have specific hours.

He turned the car into the car park at the edge of Inverness and looked at the hotel before him. It was one of the new ones. A chain, albeit an extremely posh one, and somewhere that an out-of-town tour executive might use. Mr McKinley had been in the area passing through on some personal business and Macleod thought it extremely fortunate that he was going to get to meet him so quickly.

Dressed in his suit and tie, Macleod walked into reception before scanning around to see if anyone was waiting for him. Dermot McKinley had said he'd be in the lobby from around ten o'clock. Macleod had mentioned this to a few of the constables at the station who said Dermot McKinley would be obvious due to the man's tall stature, over six feet, and broad shoulders that could swing a club.

Macleod didn't watch golf and had no idea who the man was, but the description given to him by the constables allowed him to pick out a rather gentle-looking giant sipping a coffee from a plain white cup. Macleod marched over, extending a hand and announcing himself.

'Would you be Mr. McKinley? I'm acting DCI Seoras Macleod.'

When the man stood up, Macleod felt instantly belittled. He had to actually lift his head and look up to the man's eyes, and the handshake he was given could've broken his hand on other days. Dermot McKinley seemed pleasant enough, thanked Macleod for coming out, and pointed to a seat. As Macleod sat down, he shook off the thanksgiving.

'It should be me that's thanking you, meeting me so quickly. I take it you've heard about the incident up at the golf club.'

'Newtonmoray is turning into a bigger problem than we ever thought. We're in a fantastic place here, Detective Chief Inspector.'

'Just call me Seoras,' said Macleod. 'It'll be a lot easier.'

'Well, Seoras, I'm Dermot, and as I was saying, Newton-moray is in such a wonderful location. People who come to watch golf, they're not just looking for parties and things like that. They enjoy the countryside, they enjoy tradition, they enjoy lots of places to go and see. If you're coming to a tournament up here, people will make a week of it, two weeks of it. Your tourist board will go daft, but having a killing attached to it. I take it, it is a killing, Chief Inspector.'

'Well, Dermot, obviously investigations are continuing and I'm not going to publicly announce too much, but the person in question was indeed, we believe, murdered.'

'That's disappointing,' Dermot said. 'I really love the new course. They're doing wonders with it. When I visited, I had to point out a few things with regards to how the course would be seen on camera, but nothing major. Technically, it's wonderful. I played a round on it and found it quite a challenge. Have you had a game yourself?'

'I don't play,' said Macleod. 'I'm afraid I don't really go in for a lot of sports. The games I tend to play are a lot more deadly.'

'Well, I won't say I haven't seen your face on the television, and I certainly wouldn't have traded my career in the golf course for yours, but I'll tell you, Seoras, that course is something else. It'll be a real challenge for the players coming in. I think it'll be a visual feast for the cameras. The tour and that golf club would marry up so well.'

'Can I ask,' said Macleod, 'I don't understand why they need a new course, why it was so different. Obviously, one's got lots of trees and the other doesn't.'

'Links golf,' said Dermot, 'the one without the trees as you would put it, is very traditional, but to be honest, can look very bland on the television. A lot of people now, they want big scores. They don't want the damn wind and everyone struggling badly, scrambling to make putts. Technically, links golf is a great challenge, when the wind blows, but then the wind doesn't blow and the course maybe dries out, and it becomes much, much easier. I personally think the drama on the television comes from other types of courses, but as a golfer, I want to play the links.'

Macleod shook his head. 'I won't begin to tell you I understand what you're going on about,' he said. 'What I do need to understand is the process of how you became involved and how the talks went, and what stage you're at with them.'

'Of course. The tour was initially approached by Amy Johnson. I take it you've met her. Well, I also met Sandy Mackintosh, your unfortunate victim, but I know who I'd rather talk to. She's full of life, she's good on the eye, and she knows her golf. In fairness, I had just taken up the ambassador role within the tour. They send me out to assess courses, because I know how to play, I understand what the challenges will be for our players on the tour, and I do have a background with the camera.

'The thing is that she came, and she talked about the new course all the time. New course at Newtonmoray, the Newtonmoray new course. When I played it, it was fantastic, but the old course is too. As I said before, visually and for coverage, the new course works better. So, it piqued my interest.

'Amy entered into discussions about the new course over several months. More than that, she would take me out to events, the usual soft soaping. I'll not lie to you, Seoras, one of the perks about this job is having people like her go and take you to other sporting events. We would turn up at the Open; she'd have a box over there. Football, rugby, you tell me a sport and we've probably been there to watch something, all in the name of talking about bringing us there, because it would be a big thing for the club. Massive thing.

'Amy was also very switched on. You take an event to a club like that, and suddenly all these people around the country want to go and play it. You can charge big money, during a time when a lot of courses are struggling. They need the name attached. Purists like me will go and play a course for what it's worth. I've played many courses that don't have a big name beside them, and they're fabulous. I just enjoy the course, but other people, people with money and usually less golfing sense, will charge around the country looking to play these courses that the pros have played. What she was wanting to do in bringing these people with the money to the club was marrying up what we wanted to do—bring a great product out here to another part of the world.

'The time of year we were looking to come, we wanted the inland course, because the links course could've been a little bit rough weather-wise. However, Amy said to me that recently she was struggling to get a confirmed vote. Whatever way their process was, what did she call it? Dormie, that was right. Dormie five. Anyway, they need so many people to vote through or it doesn't happen, and I think Amy had her work cut out.'

'Why do you think that was?' asked Macleod.

'People get suspicious. People are also in the club because it's their club. You don't want to turn up at your club and not be able to get out because you've got big-money-paying people on the tee ahead of you. They've also spent a lot of money on

83

that new course, and members will want to play both. You can't just relegate the members onto the links.

'I remember talking to Sandy Mackintosh, the deceased man, once. He wasn't against the new course. He just was against it being the main focus. I understood that, but in the financial world, in a place where you have to make money or you may as a club struggle, I think the links course wasn't the one to be focused on. Anyway, over the last couple of months, we've struggled to get the course confirmed on the tour. We want to go in, and Amy's kept coming back to me saying, "Can you hold off for a bit longer; can you wait for an answer?"

'I have. I've waited for a while. I'll not lie, Seoras. I enjoyed her coming to meet me. She kept taking me in for dinners and to events, but ultimately, I had to issue an ultimatum. We have deadlines to meet. We have to know what we're doing schedule-wise. It may be several years down the line, but that doesn't stop us from needing to have plans in place. The locality must know. All the accommodation must be ready. Any transport links that need beefed up have to be done. Hosting one of these events is not a simple thing. We will be years in advance. The decision happening now has a massive effect. I told her, because I held out for too long really, that the vote needed passed in two weeks or the deal was off. We were going to walk away.'

'Just walk away?' asked Macleod, 'You really would just forget it after all that work.'

'Yes. This is not the only club vying for a date on the tour and we're not just talking here in the UK, we're talking Europe. They're lucky enough that the timeframe was there. We needed a club. It's got to be UK at these dates. We do have a few others we'd look out, but Newtonmoray's the number one. All they've got to do is sign.'

The big man bent down and picked up his coffee cup, taking a long drink. Then he placed it back down and stared at Macleod.

'This is the problem, it's not run like a business. A golf club needs to have that business acumen. Even its Operations Manager didn't get that.'

'You met the whole board, I take it,' said Macleod.

'Every one of them.'

'How big a loss would it be to you if they didn't get the vote?' asked Macleod.

'Personally, yes, it would be a loss. Put a lot of time into this. The biggest loss ever would be for them, but the tour will find somewhere else. We'll go somewhere else, and it'll be a success. It might not be exactly what we want, but there's always the week after. There's plenty of dates on the calendar.

'It would be a massive loss for Amy. She put an awful lot of work into it. Can you imagine she wants to take somebody like me off to this event, that event, back to dinner, keeping me talking? She's a slip of a girl by comparison to me. The two of us, we're from different eras. I was divorced six years ago, Seoras. Not easy to find company. Always on the move, always here, there, and wherever, and well, I won't pay for company in that sense. I didn't have any designs other than a nice evening or a trip to a sporting event. It was that simple, but Amy, she really wanted this.

'I think she felt if she could do for this club then she can move on in the golf world and do it for other places. It'd be a heck of a prize for her because it'd be her baby. It'd be Amy that did it. The club may bask in the glory of having the tour, but she would be the one getting the credit behind the scenes.

She would be the one that anybody else looking for that sort of level of expertise would notice. They will be looking at her, not at the Chairman, not at the other officers of the club.'

'This might seem a strange question,' said Macleod, 'but in your time there, would you have seen anything that would cause anyone to act in such a violent manner towards Sandy Mackintosh?'

'No. Everybody's nice as pie when people like me come round,' said Dermot. 'You don't want to show any particular problems. Sandy was a little bit different, and yes, he told me flat, we should be on the links course. I told him why we shouldn't; he argued back, but it was all friendly. I didn't see anyone looking at him with daggers or showing any dissent in front of me, but like I say, you don't do that. Not in front of the customer, so to speak.'

'How long has the club got before you pull out?'

'We said two weeks. Well, now you're down to a week, and well, we might be able to push it a little bit but not much with what's happening. It is awkward though because publicity won't be good. We're talking far enough in the future that if this is the only murder around and it's not tied to the club, not associated with the club other than it actually happened there, well, we can sign the deal. We can announce in a year when people have forgotten most of what's going on.'

'What if it is associated with the club? What if it is to do with this issue?'

'How will that ever come out? Well, being cold about it, only if it came out would we really have a problem. Can you imagine? We're going back to the course that somebody died at. Somebody was killed to bring this competition there. That isn't going to work for our sponsors. It's not going to work for us and it's not going to work for me, but in all honesty, I don't think that is the case. I can't see people getting to that level. We're all lovers of the game.'

'Maybe,' said Macleod, 'but when there's money at stake, in my experience, people will do a lot of things.'

'Maybe I'm just a little bit too kind to people then,' said Dermot, 'but understand this, that if the publicity goes negative, we're out. It won't happen.'

Macleod sat back and watched as the man drank more coffee. He had thought about getting one himself, but it looked rather disappointing and he didn't want to sit with a poor coffee.

He was done really. He should have thanked Dermot and then disappeared back to the office, but he didn't want to go back. There were some overtime forms sitting and there was a calculation to be made around the previous months. He also had to pull out some new working patterns that were going to be discussed, and right now, he didn't want to go near it. Right now, he wanted to do what he used to do, sit and think, go and interview people.

He was having to keep himself away from Hope, having to let her shine, and it wasn't easy. Over the last while, they had built up such a great team. They worked well together and now they wanted to bump them all up. Move them all up a place as if it wouldn't change anything, but, of course, it would change something.

It was a different role. The team would become more Hope's than his, and what he couldn't do was occupy that space and not let her move up. She deserved it. She had a whole career ahead of her. What did he have? A couple of years? If even that. The way he felt about the DCI job at the moment, he might go even earlier. No. He would stay here for a while. He would stay here because it was better than doing any of that paperwork.

'Tell me a bit more about links and parkland golf,' said Macleod. 'I just want a lot more background and understanding.'

'In what way?' asked Dermot.

'You talked about the cameras and things. A few more specifics would really help.'

Macleod sat back in his chair, having avoided the paperwork back at the office for another little while, and the not unsmooth voice of Dermot McKinley chewed over the intricacies of how to make a contoured green appear spectacular on a television screen.

Chapter 10

'**H**e's ready for you.'

Hope looked up at Clarissa standing in her boots, tartan trews, and a shawl wrapped around her.

'Are you going to wear that in the interview room?' asked Hope. 'Does it not feel too warm?'

'The day a place becomes too warm for a spot of class like this,' said Clarissa, 'will be the day hell freezes over. Are you ready?'

'Coming now,' said Hope. She marched off behind Clarissa towards a small office that had been put aside to do the interviews of the board members. Alastair Begley was always going to be at the club, being the Chief Operating Officer. He volunteered to be the first one to be interviewed by the pair of them after other constables had been employed in taking down the mundane details of their movements. Hope had been reading through these submissions. Alastair Begley had no alibi for the time of Sandy Mackintosh's death, but there was nothing to indicate he was in the area either. Something that was too common with most of them, for only Amy Johnson seemed to have an alibi.

As Hope turned the corner and followed Clarissa into the small office, she saw sitting behind a desk the gangly figure of Alastair Begley. He kept biting his nails as if worried and Hope asked if he wanted a coffee before they sat down. Hope turned to the constable who had been manning the door, and he was dispatched bringing back coffees a few minutes later. Once the door was closed, Hope nodded to Clarissa that they could start the interview proper.

'Mr Begley,' said Hope, 'we understand that you're against the new course. You spoke to me previously. Can you just flesh that out a bit? From what I understand, if a deal is done with the tour company, there's potentially money in it, money that's going to help the club, money that's going to maybe make the club. You could be a big fish in the water instead of maybe only being . . .' Words failed Hope. Then she heard a cough from a colleague beside her.

'A medium trout,' said Clarissa. Hope shot her a look. *How did that work? A medium trout?*

'Forgive me, ladies,' said Begley, 'but I don't think you understand. I know what you do, but you're not getting the picture.'

'Well, fill us in,' said Clarissa; 'always happy to learn.'

'This old course we have out on the links, it's a classic, but it needs to be maintained. It's been around for a long time; the environment causes damage. We have various areas that are going to need shored up because of the inclement weather we've been having. We're getting heavier rainfalls, we're getting drier patches, just less and less consistency to when we can expect the weather as well. You then get increased throughput at times. Greens need manicured, they need looked after, they need lifted on occasion, and reset. It all takes money.

'The new one, it eats money. While we were building it, it

was like a devouring beast. People think we're in a really good position. They look out, they see the cars at the club. They see the restaurant, the events. We're lucky to be cutting even. It's a problem that Amy has produced with her fancy dreams.'

'You sound quite resentful towards her,' said Clarissa.

'Well, yes!' said Begley. 'Her job was to come in and help this golf club. Her idea of helping it, is to take away the soul of it.'

'How do you mean exactly?' asked Hope.

'Well, like I've said before, she fills people's heads with dreams of tournament golf. About the big draw or thrill of bringing someone here. She talks about hotels in the area, and that, and how they'll be filling the local economy. That's not us, local economy is not us. What do we get paid for hosting it? What do we get out of the ticket sales of the people that come? What do we get from the TV revenue? Not enough, not enough for the hassle it's going to cause, and at the same time, you're going to have a course that's going to have to be taken apart. A course that's going to take all the money that we have, and the old course is going to get left behind. The members aren't going to be on that new course. Oh, no, they'll be kept off so the fairways and flower beds can be made to look special. We'll get it in the rough months if we're lucky when there'll be temporary greens.'

Hope looked over at Clarissa.

'When the weather's bad,' said Clarissa, 'you don't use the greens, that's the bit at the end of the flag. You go off it. You cut a big hole in a bucket, and you play on to what's called a temporary green but it's not proper greens. It's just part of the fairway.'

Hope wasn't sure that she understood what was being said

91

but indicated that Begley should continue. 'If I'm honest,' he said, 'the numbers are tight. Running a golf course like this, running a club, we're not making lots of money—we're struggling. She was brought in to help with initiatives to getting more people playing, more people as part of the club. You want people to join the club so for the year you know you're covered. You know roughly what money is coming in. We don't want these pay-to-play people.'

Hope flashed a look over at Clarissa again.

'Pay-to-play people turn up once, they pay their money, they play a round. What Mr Begley's wanting is people who will commit to the year for the club so the club knows they've got a certain amount of money coming in. I would imagine it's quite significant for a company or a club like this.'

'Yes. I mean, we've done our best to try and include other people,' said Begley, 'but you do need to have a bit of money to play here.'

'And you were probably thinking about weekday golfers, in-centivising that sort of way, possibly Bring a Friend discounts for the members to try and build the membership, society days. Something that the club would use, not something where the club steps out of way and other people come and use the club.'

'That it exactly,' said Begley, 'she'll destroy the soul. The club should be for the members. She's talking about them being kicked out, not catered in the small scale by the restaurant. The club members have first access; that's the way it should be done. They do bring in other things. We have lots of people who are members of other organisations who come for golf days. That's what it should be for, not just somebody who rolls up. She will have us selling golf tee times on the internet. The providers would take a cut off that, and by the time everything comes through, trust me, the money is not as good as it looks. She was brought in here to help the club, but if she's not careful she'll end up ruining it. That's why I don't want to vote for the tour to come in. The tour will drop you as quick as they take you on.

'The investment that has to go into getting that course up to scratch to make a championship course is enormous, and then the tour will come in, they'll maybe have one, two years, three, they'll probably not commit to more than that. Then, lo and behold, they pull out, and you still haven't recouped your money. Who's going to cover it then? All the members. The members will look at their new fees, and they'll go, "This is ridiculous;" off they'll go, join somewhere else. We're not all loaded with money. We're not all able to afford any price the club sets.'

'You haven't much good to say about Amy,' said Clarissa.

'When she came,' said Begley, 'I sat down with her, I tried to work with her, and she seemed charming. She can turn a head; she's that age, and a lot of us that lurk around here, are heading to the old fart department, but I did try to help her. I thought we could do with some enthusiasm, some young blood to look at things from a different angle, but she's not a golfer.'

'Why would that make a big difference?' asked Hope.

Begley looked at her as if she'd asked the most incomprehensible question the world had ever heard.

'Forgive my colleague,' said Clarissa. 'Sergeant, what the Chief Operating Officer's trying to say is that she's taking away what makes golf, golf. She's taking away the essence, the friendships, the banter, the joy of their own course, taking somebody else around it, showing it off. She's turning it into a commodity that you pay to go and use.'

'Exactly,' said Begley. 'Exactly.'

When they exited the interview room, Hope stopped Clarissa outside. 'All that stuff he's talking about; essence, soul of the club, and whatever, how much of a driving factor would that be in him?'

'Do you mean, would he kill for it?' asked Clarissa.

'I guess ultimately, yes, I am asking that.'

'Well, yes, he probably would, or at least there's always that potential, but he'd have no need to, he had no need to at all.'

'No, but it would certainly throw a spanner in the works, you start bumping people off.'

'Never thought about that like that,' said Clarissa, 'I was thinking the motive would be to replace, get your five versus two instead of the two versus five that they had. Either that or get rid of her.'

'Take five,' said Hope. 'Then we'll be in with the Club Chairman. I think it could be a bit more interesting.'

'Well, he's got a lot to gain, hasn't he? From Sandy Mackintosh's passing.'

'We'll see,' said Hope, and disappeared back to her desk. She quickly scanned through reports, got a hold of Ross, and pushed him for an update on the CCTV. She also phoned Jona who calmly told her that when she had something for her, she'd get a hold of her. Hope sat back in her seat.

She was chasing them up, checking on them. Is that what Seoras did? Did he do it quite like that? Was he much more relaxed? I mean he did chin her at times; he did come in and ask.

Five minutes later, Hope and Clarissa were back in the same room, but with Andrew Peters, the Club Chairman, opposite them. He was in a shirt. His sleeves rolled up, tie undone, and he looked terrible.

'Are you all right?' asked Hope. 'Don't take this the wrong way, Mr Peters, but you look rough.'

'I didn't get much sleep last night,' he said. 'This whole thing, it's playing on my mind.'

'And why is that?' asked Clarissa.

'I was recently bereaved,' he said. 'My wife passed on not very long ago at all. And now one of my best friends has just died. We used to be close, my Annie and Sandy with his Dolina. It brings back a lot of memories being up at the club. We used to come up for dinners, used to be here all the time. I'd be out playing rounds with Sandy. The two women also came up to play in four balls a lot. Sandy was quite decent at one point playing with my Annie. They even went away to a few tournaments. A big part of my life disappeared. I'm afraid, last night I probably drank a bit too much.

'Well, that's understandable,' said Clarissa, 'but as long as you're up to answering questions.'

'I'll do my best,' he said.

'Well, the first is, why did you bring Amy Johnson in?' asked Hope.

'For the club,' said Peters, 'obviously for the club. We needed to boost the club's image. Were we getting by? Barely. Numbers were diminishing. Oh, ten, fifteen years ago, I wanted to bring a new course. Well, we got that through and approved, but it was a fight. Then I needed someone who could sell it. I needed someone who could make it come alive. People would look and think 'Newtonmoray' and associate it as not just being another links course. That's where we were, in the magazines, you know. 'Go to Scotland, tour this area, tour that way.' We were there on a circuit of links courses, number four or five. The one you go and play if you've got an extra day if you're lucky. Not one you were coming to, and that wasn't fair, it's not fair on that course because that's a damn fine links course.'

'Why do you think it didn't get the recognition it deserved?' asked Hope.

'It just wasn't sold right. We brought in John Henshaw initially, but to be honest, after a couple of years, he'd got nowhere. I got introduced to Amy when I was away at a friend's course down in England. She'd been working for them as the junior, but the Publicity Officer down there raved about her. She wanted her own place, she wanted her own chance to stand on her own two feet. She was keen, wanted to show the world what she could do. And then, when I met her, well, you've seen her, she's incredibly engaging, but I didn't pick her because of the way she looks. I picked her because of the way she thinks, and she's done wonders. We've got the tour practically ready to come. All we've got to do is sign it.

'The hard bit's been getting these people, a lot of whom I love, to understand what this club needs. I'm having to drag it into the next century. The old models, the old ways of doing golf clubs, they don't exist anymore. Or at least they're not working well. We need to be able to cover ourselves. We need to keep ourselves current. Keep ourselves at the front. Have a name. Newtonmoray needs to be the golf club you go to. It'll be on the tour. They'll come and play it. The design of it's good, very good. Dermot McKinley, who we deal with from the tour, he loved it. He's an ex-player, fabulous player. Did you ever see him play?'

'A few times,' said Clarissa. 'Quite an upright striker of the ball, if I remember.'

'That's it, but he's so tall, isn't he?'

Hope felt like the conversation was flying in front of her eyes, but she wasn't really that involved.

'Amy's the one who's done all that with him. Amy's the one who's kept him here. She's the one who's fought for us to have this time to sort out a proper vote. The tour should be out of here by now with the response that my board has given.'

'What makes you think they'll change?' asked Hope.

'I don't know. We just need to keep going.'

'You didn't ever think about moving people out of the way?'

'What do you mean?' asked Peters.

'Well, with your policy that you have to achieve a dormie five, you have to get five people on board. You were two against five. Did you ever think about how to remove them? How you were going to get past this roadblock you seem to have?'

'I really did think,' he said, 'that I could convince them, but I'm weary of the fighting. Now, I've lost Sandy, my friend, but the club goes on, it has to, as much as I'm pained by his death.'

Hope looked at the man, and the eyes seemed to be welling.

'Maybe it was something ordained from above,' said Peters. 'Maybe he was meant to go. Maybe he was meant to make way for someone else. We've got two people standing soon for his post. We need to get the vote done because we need to make a proper official vote on whether or not we accept the tour's conditions.'

'Who are the two that are standing?' asked Hope.

'Well, I've just been finalising that. John Durbin and Marion Linwood. John would back us to the hilt; he loves the idea of the tour being here. Marion's more like Sandy was. The thing is Marion's very well-liked as well. Most of the members are not aware of the real debate going on, and the finances. They like Marion, she's a lovely person but stuck in the past like the rest of them. You see, it wasn't a case of just bump somebody off and then fill them with my cronies. It doesn't work like that. Sometimes you have to hope for a bit of luck, when in truth, I think, me and Amy are out of it. It's sad to say we could be turning down what could be the rescue of this club.'

When the man left the interview room, Hope thought he looked defeated with a sorrow in him for his friend. She was quite surprised there wasn't the same fire in him to drive forward the cause anymore.

'What do you make of him?' asked Hope.

Clarissa stood looking at the door the man had just walked out of. She gave a shake of her head. 'Dreamer gone wrong,' she said. 'I get the thing about his wife and his friend, but he seemed to have big dreams here. Big dreams have been ruined. In my mind that makes him dangerous. Makes him a risk.'

'You really think so? You really think he could be like that?'

'You don't know golf,' said Clarissa. 'You really don't.'

Chapter 11

It had been a long night for Alan Ross sat in front of his screens, searching through the local CCTV cameras with two constables beside him. One looked as if she'd barely got out of college, but the other was a grumpy, older man. They were fine at what they did, but they were not great company. The older man complained a lot, and Ross noted that he seemed to have that stomach trouble that people had on night shift. Your system never worked the same. That was the problem. There were several belches and burps that broke the silence as they worked.

The woman on his right-hand side, who he thought could only have been twenty-one, maybe twenty-two, seemed to be forever going down to buy a chocolate bar from the machine down in the canteen. Ross counted. She went down and up ten times during the night. Not once did she ask him if he wanted anything. However, they did their job, and it was because of that, that Ross was able to come up with some rather interesting information.

The first thing he had done was get a constable to collect the car details of all the members of the board. They were just individuals they were interested in, and so he thought that scanning the CCTV might help pick up their movements. After all, he was verifying their cars in the only way he could, for they had no other alibis.

The car of Pádraig O'Reilly appeared on the CCTV at around ten o'clock in the morning for Ross. Of course, it was during the morning of the murder in the time on the screen. Ross's eyes were drooping at that point, but he spotted it. The car passed close to the course, but there was no footage of the man stopping. However, an hour later, he was seen driving back the other way.

Given the locale of the CCTV cameras, there was a possibility that the car could have been parked somewhere, but there was also the possibility that the car could have gone into a small estate. After all, Orla Smith's house was on that estate, but her car was never seen departing or leaving, and she couldn't be seen walking anywhere. However, it was enough to question Pádraig O'Reilly. The man had claimed not to have been out that morning.

By the time they checked through all the detail, and gathered it into a nice package on his phone to then take up to Hope, it was getting closer to ten o'clock. He remembered she was doing the interviews this morning of the board and on calling, he found out that Pádraig O'Reilly was not due in until at least midday. He decided this was worth a proper visit to the club, and so he jumped into his car and drove up on a rather cold morning.

There was snow in the clouds, but none was falling presently, and that which had fallen previously was slowly disappearing. When he entered the clubhouse, he found that Hope had just finished interviewing the Chairman, and he tracked her down to the desk she'd been working at for most of the night.

'Morning, Alan,' she said. 'You seem excited.'

Ross was excited. He'd cracked it, or at least something. He liked it when that happened.

He always thought of Macleod or Hope like a dog. If he could find them the right toy, if he could dig it out for them and toss it to them, they then spent the next hour or two wrestling with it. It was not an image that he shared with them however, but it was the truth.

'I've got something for you,' said Ross. 'Pádraig O'Reilly, caught him on CCTV the morning of the murder. He's passing by close to the course in his car, comes back an hour later. It equates unfavourably for him compared to when the murder happened. Just time for him within that point to park the car up, get on to the course, do what has to be done and come back. He also said he wasn't out that morning.'

'That's right,' said Hope, 'he did, didn't he?'

Ross put his phone down on the desk in front of Hope and played the images. 'That's his grey car there,' said Ross. 'You see the timeframe when he went through, and you see it when he came back. Plenty of opportunity to commit the murder.'

'Yet he doesn't stop.'

'Well, not there,' said Ross, 'but he must have stopped somewhere, you don't drive around for an hour there. Where the CCTV cameras are, he can't get out of that area. He would've been picked up if his car had left. The only thing he can be is in that area with the car. And what's he doing? He had no reason not to tell us.'

Hope stood up, suddenly grabbed her jacket and flung it around her. 'Stay on here,' she said. 'Join Clarissa interviewing the rest of the board members. She'll bring you up to speed. Let her take the questions. I'm off to see O'Reilly.'

'Do you not want me to come with you to O'Reilly?' asked Ross.

'No, you can't. We've got board members coming in. O'Reilly wasn't meant to be in until twelve but I'm not hanging on this. I'm going to see him now. He's become lead suspect but we can't ignore those coming in already for interviews, so get on it with Clarissa. I'll speak to you soon, Ross.'

He watched as Hope went to leave, then she stopped at the door and turned around.

'It's good work as ever, Alan. Top stuff. We wouldn't be where we are without you and your speed of work.'

She looked tired as she turned, and despite the scar that ran across her face, Ross thought that Hope usually carried an incredible grace and bearing and a beauty with it. However, this morning she looked tired, worn down. He hoped that her wrestling with the toy this morning would bring some sort of joy for her.

* * *

Accompanied by a constable, Hope drove to Pádraig O'Reilly's house. It was on a small estate not far from Newtonmoray and everything seemed to be a new build. That was getting to be the way around the Inverness area. Lots and lots of houses going up and more and more people coming. Some of the people at the station said it was ruining the landscape. The place had changed so much in the last twenty years, they barely recognised it. Hope hadn't been up here that long and she thought it was good for the area, so much vibrancy. The rest of the UK wasn't the same.

They parked outside the house, walked down the tarmac

driveway, and stood at the semi-detached house with a bottle-green front door. It had a fancy-looking porch, except that Hope saw it as cheaper timber, not solid; after pressing the brass bell, she stood and waited. The door opened with a small woman carrying a baby in her arms. The child was gurgling, but the woman's eyes were fixed on Hope, and they seemed pensive.

'Paddy said there was trouble up at the golf club; are you here about that?'

Hope pulled out a warrant card. 'I'm Detective Sergeant Hope McGrath. This is Constable Finlay beside me. We're just here to ask Pádraig some questions. Would he be at home?'

'Yeah, he's home. Hang on a minute.' She turned and shouted up the stairs. 'Paddy, get your arse down here. Police are here for you.'

There were screams from upstairs. Hope thought she heard a child cry, but amidst all the chaos, she saw Pádraig O'Reilly march his way down the stairs to stand beside his wife.

'Sergeant,' he said, 'what's going on?'

'Is there somewhere we can talk privately?'

'You can say what you want in front of me,' said his wife.

Hope looked at Pádraig and he nodded.

'Okay then,' said Hope. 'Yesterday morning, when Sandy Mackintosh was being killed, we have your car passing CCTV cameras that place you close enough to the course. You said to me you didn't leave the house yesterday; you were coming in later and yet you're out in your car. Can you explain that, please?'

'He was out getting a spot of shopping. That's what he said,' his wife said.

'Where did you shop then?' asked Hope and saw the man's

face screwing up. 'I'm sorry, but I need to ask you again. Where were you shopping?'

'I didn't want to do this in front of Mandy here, but the thing is, I popped out to buy something as a surprise for her. The thing is that when I went to the house I'd bought it from—I had purchased it off eBay—it wasn't available anymore. They'd taken it all down, didn't want to part with it.'

Hope thought the man looked edgy. 'What is it that you went to buy?'

'It's not going to be much of a pissing surprise, is it, if I stand here and tell you it now?'

His wife looked at him. Hope could sense that she was almost ready to be more of a detective than Hope was. 'Damn it, Paddy, just tell them. Just damn well tell her. Get them off our backs. He's meant to be in today at twelve anyway with you lot. What are you doing out here now?'

'Excuse me, Mandy,' said Hope, 'but Mr O'Reilly, can you please tell me what the item was? Can you give me the address you went to?'

The man looked at her. He was silent.

'Paddy, for God's sake, just tell her. I don't care, all right? I don't care what it is. I don't care. I'll forget about it. You can just buy me some flowers or whatever it is, whatever you're buying me stuff for, but just damn well tell them.'

The man remained quiet. 'Where was this item to be picked up from?' asked Hope again. 'What were the names of the people? Can you show me on your phone or on your laptop where you initially bought the item on eBay?'

Again, Pádraig remained quiet. His wife's baby now started to scream, and she held the child close, but her eyes never left her husband.

'Just damn well tell them, Paddy. What harm's there going to be telling them? You can't just stand here and not say anything to them. How's that going to look? Don't worry about me. I've told you, I don't care if it's a crap present. I don't care if it's . . . well, whatever it is. Just tell them where it was so they can scrub you out of this nonsense.

'You know Paddy wouldn't have done anything to that man. He liked Sandy. Sandy Mackintosh and Paddy were on the same side. The pair of them kept telling them all up there with their nonsense. He's a proper golfer, you see, my Paddy. My Paddy's a proper golfer. Knows all about it. Not like them up there. What's that woman up there called?'

'Amy,' said Pádraig almost automatically.

'Yes, that Amy bird, dressed up to the nines and all that, look at her. Turned his head, and Andrew Peter's head's been turned. His wife's gone you see, that's the problem. Everybody needs a good person standing beside them. Now Paddy's got me. He's got me stood beside him.'

'Mr O'Reilly, kindly tell me the address you went to; otherwise, I'll be forced to continue this conversation at the station,' said Hope.

Pádraig O'Reilly stood motionless, and Hope thought he was almost looking past her. There was a strain across his face while his wife was egging him to speak. Hope waited. She gave another warning a minute later.

'I'm waiting, Mr O'Reilly. I'm waiting or we go downtown.'

'What's the problem, Paddy? Just tell them. If you were going to buy something, it'll be on eBay. I'll go and get my laptop.'

'Don't,' he said, but it was too late as his wife strode off and came back two minutes later with a laptop in one hand, the baby still in the other.

'Here we go,' she said, and placed it on a small table beside the door. She flicked it up, tapped a couple of numbers when the lock screen came up, and then clicked on the icon to search the internet for eBay. Once she had got in, it had automatically come up with a link and soon she was typing into eBay looking for the past purchases.

'That's funny,' she said. 'There's nothing here, Paddy, what did you . . .'

'I told you I didn't want it.'

'But that's not going to stop it from being here. Hang on,' she said. Then she stood up and looked at him. His eyes were almost glazed over. 'What have you been up to?' she said. 'What have you been up to?' and then her left hand swung, despite the baby being held in the right, and caught Pádraig O'Reilly smack across the cheek. Hope could hear the crack, seeing it as one of the strongest slaps she'd ever known. 'You dirty sod,' said Mandy. 'You dirty, dirty sod. What were you at? Where were you?'

'I think we'll continue this formally down at the station. Constable, do the formalities, please.' The constable stepped forward and Hope made a beeline for Mandy O'Reilly. She could see the tears coming down the woman's eyes.

'Is there anyone I can call? Is there anyone else I can bring here? You don't look in a state to be left alone.'

'Five kids,' said Mandy suddenly, tears falling from her face. 'Five kids and he's off doing whatever. You better take him in,' she said. 'You better take him in, because if he stays here, he'll be singing bloody soprano.'

Hope heard the constable over her shoulder speaking to O'Reilly and then leading him down to the car. Hope would need some help. Ross and Clarissa were tied up doing the other board members, so she picked up the phone and dialled into the station. She found the call diverted, however, before Macleod picked it up.

'I hope you're not busy,' she said. 'We've got our first suspect.'

'Looking promising then. Who is it?'

'O'Reilly,' said Hope, 'I need you to come in and sit in on the interview with me.'

'Not a problem,' said Macleod, 'but it's not him. Makes no sense.'

'No, but he's the only one in the area and he's holding something back. Half an hour please, Seoras, if that suits you.'

Hope turned and walked out the door, hearing it slam shut hard behind her. *Five kids and a husband like that*, she thought. *How do you go from someone like me to someone in that position?*

As she climbed into the car, Pádraig O'Reilly was quiet in the back. Hope let the constable drive off and she turned and looked at the man. He showed no sign of emotion. She could see him having been up to something, but she thought Macleod was right. This wasn't a murderer. She felt he was more pro-life than a lot of people.

Chapter 12

Hope opened the door of Macleod's office, a file under her arm. She swept her eyes this way and that, realising that the inspector wasn't behind his desk. 'Seoras, are you in?' asked Hope.

'Down in the corner. Where did he keep these files?'

Hope strode into the room, turned, and looked down at Macleod on his knees, rummaging through the filing system. He had the bottom drawer out, pushing A4 folders back and forward while scanning.

'Are you ready for this interview? He's definitely holding something back.'

'Yeah. Not as much as this is. Where did he put those rosters? I have no idea how this works. I've been a detective for how long and I can't find a darn thing in here.'

'Seoras, we need to go.'

'Okay, okay, just give me a minute.'

She watched Macleod stand up and thought he was slower these days. He crossed the office, opened a side door into a smaller office where a woman sat behind a desk.

'Can you find those rosters for me?'

'Of course, Seoras. Not a problem, I did explain the system

to you.'

'I think you could explain the system to me until the cows come home. It'll never be my system and I won't find it. Just leave them out on the desk when you've got them. No rush, I've got to go into interview now anyway.'

He closed the door behind him and held out a hand, letting Hope walk in front of him.

'There's no need to be chivalrous,' she said.

'I'm not. This is your investigation, you're lead investigator, you go in first. I'll not be saying much unless you need me to.'

'You never told me to play it like that.'

'You were never my boss,' said Macleod, 'but for the record, I never cut you off from asking questions.'

'I never said you did, but you never told me to hold back, and I never did.'

'No, you didn't, and now we're having a little argument about something that's nothing. Just go and do what you do, I'll back you up.'

Hope smiled and marched off down the corridor, realising by the time she had reached the end of it, Macleod was at least five or six paces behind.

'Why do they make it like that? Why do they make it so complicated? There's got to be an easier way.'

'Seoras, I don't want to hear about your rosters. I've got enough to do. Head in the game, please.' Macleod flicked his eyes up at Hope and she realised that she'd probably said too much.

'My head is always in the game, but I take your point.'

Hope turned back again, walking down the last corridor before opening the door into where O'Reilly sat accompanied by a constable. Hope sat down, watched Macleod sit beside her and the constable leave. She put out in front of her the small file she was carrying and flipped open the front cover. She was aware Macleod was staring at her and then she realised what hadn't happened. There was no coffee. Well, she wasn't stopping an interview for coffee.

'How well did you know Sandy Mackintosh?' asked Hope.

'Knew him as well as anyone else,' said O'Reilly. 'Proper golfer. Always there to give you tips and advice. Saw eye to eye on this, the latest row.'

'I'm aware of that,' said Hope. 'What about other things at the club?'

'Like what?'

'Did you ever disagree on anything?'

'Sandy thought that the water sprinkling system on the third hole of the new course showed some poor placement because the sprinkler heads were up too close to the edge of the green. With the approach shot that would come in, the likelihood of the ball landing in that area was high. You were also liable to get a drop because of some of the sprinkler heads that they used and put in. I disagreed, but I'm not sure it's enough for murder.'

'Be serious,' said Hope. 'Mr O'Reilly, we have a dead man here.'

'I've got a dead friend and by the looks of it somebody's bumped him off so they can get this stupid course through, and I wouldn't go to that sort of length. I'm on his side. It's wholly ridiculous that you've got me in here.'

'Then where were you going?'

'I told you, I was getting something for the wife, only it was wrong.'

'What were you getting for the wife?'

The man shook his head. 'Just a gift.'

How long do you think you've been in here?' said Macleod suddenly.

'Feels like at least three hours.'

Macleod glanced at his watch. 'Two and a half. You and the wife, are you part of the same social group?' asked Macleod. 'I mean have you got friends who are husbands of her friends? Are you at that age when they sort of get the couple's connection, so to speak, or with kids, you know each other from the schools and that?'

'Probably know a few; yes, I would say most of us are.'

'Interesting,' said Macleod. He sat back in his chair and smiled at Hope.

How was that interesting? Hope thought. 'What's your opinion of the tour coming? Would you not like it to come to the club?'

'Of course, I'd love to see the players, but it causes a lot of hassle. I've been at other clubs before. Major issue, depends on what you want your club to be. Mackintosh wanted it to be a club for people there. Social aspect, everything like that. You bring these people in and you make it a course that people pay to play. They come in from here, there, and wherever; they expect buggies, they expect special restaurants. They expect people wandering around with hot dogs out on the course, paying through the nose for it, corporate piling in and suddenly you don't get many members.

'They won't like it if we're all relegated to our links, because most golfers . . . most golfers like the variation. The idea of having two golf courses at a club, both very different, that attracts people, even if the fee is slightly high. That's because you've got plenty of opportunity, plenty of options.'

There was a knock at the door, and the constable came in and whispered in Hope's ear. A friend of O'Reilly's was at the front desk and asking to see her. The desk sergeant had put him into a different room.

'If you excuse us for a moment, Mr O'Reilly; it appears that someone may be coming to your aid.'

Hope stood up and Macleod followed her out of the door. As she walked down the corridor, having let the constable return to the room to sit with O'Reilly, Hope said quietly, 'What was all that about? Type of family he's got, who their friends are?'

'Two and a half hours. This is going to be one of his friends saying that Pádraig came round to visit them. He's going to be buying something off him but it's not going to be right. If you notice that O'Reilly has not said a word about what it was, he hasn't said where he's gone, so this guy is a plant. This will be beautiful; watch this.'

Hope turned into the new room where a different constable was sitting with a gaunt-looking man, maybe in his forties.

'Good afternoon,' said Hope. 'Who are you?'

'My name is Ivan Greene, I think there might be a bit of confusion with Mr O'Reilly. You see, he came round to my house yesterday.'

'And where do you live?' asked Hope. She wasn't terribly surprised when the man gave an address that sat in between the CCTV cameras that O'Reilly had been spotted on. 'What was Mr O'Reilly doing there today?' asked Hope.

'He's been looking for a while to buy some crystal for his wife and I said I had some. But when he came around, it's the wrong series. That's the trouble with it, isn't it? Waterford, Tyrone, all these different types of crystal wherever you go. Oh, you don't know what series is what? You don't know when it came out. He had a look at mine, and it wasn't the right thing. Headed home. Of course, he didn't want his wife to know.

'And you thought you should come here because?'

'Well, he's been brought in.'

'That's right. When exactly did he come to see you?'

'Yesterday morning it was.'

'I take it you've heard then about what happened on the golf course,' said Hope.

'Well, there's been a murder,' said the man. 'Golf Course Killer, that's what they're calling it.'

Macleod leaned over and whispered in Hope's ear. 'I specifically told them not to use those words. The tour isn't going to be happy.'

'What made you think we were bringing Mr O'Reilly in here to do with the murder?'

The man looked first at Macleod and then at Hope. 'You're having a laugh, aren't you?' said Mr Greene. 'It's you, Sergeant McGrath and Macleod, Murder Team, Inverness. You brought him in. What else is it going to be about? You don't do traffic violations.'

Macleod stood up and put his hand out to the man. The man shook it looking bemusedly at Macleod.

'Believe it or not,' said Macleod. 'You're not actually wasting our time. If anything, you've helped us to no end. Thank you very much for coming in and for passing on that information. I must caution you. Next time, do not lie to the police. Even if you think it can help your friend. We'll let it slide this time though.'

The man stood bemused as Macleod shook his hand and then turned and walked out. Hope stood up, not quite sure what to do for a moment. Then she turned to the constable.

'Escort Mr Greene back off the premises and Mr Greene, you heard what the DCI said.' She had to run up to catch up with Macleod as he strode down the corridor. 'What was that?' she said. 'You can't talk to people like that.'

'Oh, you can,' he said. 'Especially when they come in lying through their teeth like that, but we'll go in, tell O'Reilly what his friend has said. He'll then look to leave but don't let him. You go after him. Mr Greene coming in has just cut off about three or four hours of messing about with O'Reilly.'

'I thought you weren't taking over. I thought this was mine to run.'

Macleod stopped dead in the corridor, stood back to one side and held his hand out to allow Hope to walk in front. 'Sorry,' he said. 'Just pitching in to help.'

Together they both marched back to the room holding O'Reilly, who wore a broad smile as they walked in.

'You've got plenty of friends, Pádraig, haven't you?' said Hope. 'Fortunately, one of them has come along, a Mr Greene, do you know where Mr Greene lives?'

'Ivan. Yes, I know where Ivan lives. That's where I went. I went to Ivan's.'

'What were you looking at in Ivan's? It's okay. He's told us so you can tell us.'

'Well, for the wife I was getting . . . yes, it's curtains. Curtains that Ivan had.'

'He said crystal. Apparently, you've had trouble getting hold of crystal.' Hope watched O'Reilly almost curse himself. 'Where were you?' asked Hope. 'When I was stood at your house, your wife was freaking out. Your wife was having a go at you. At first, I thought it was you getting arrested, but I think it might be something else. Something you can't want her to know. Something that's going to blow the two of you apart if it's admitted to.'

O'Reilly slumped back in his chair.

'You'll need to come out with it,' said Macleod, 'because it'll come out eventually and at some point, she's going to come in here.'

Hope glanced sideways at Macleod. 'Who was she? How did he know that she would come in?'

'That's the trouble. Especially when it's an attachment. Especially when it's more than just meeting up, more than just sex. This is what happens when there's a connection formed,' said Macleod. 'Trouble with connections is they show in public. You don't think they do. You don't hold hands, you don't stare at each other. In fact, sometimes you mess it up because you go the other way and try and keep away or at least you do. Your illicit partner doesn't. Oh no, she stares more intently. She puts little glances in, especially when you're under pressure. Especially when you're stressed. You can tell me who she is. I think she lives in the area, doesn't she?'

Hope looked over. The numbers suddenly clicking in her head.

'Why were you at Orla Smith's?' said Hope.

'Because he's right,' said O'Reilly. 'I can't say because when it comes out in the open properly, well then, Mandy will hit the roof properly. There'll be hell to pay. Can't do that with that many kids dependent on me.'

'We'd need to confirm that though,' said Hope, 'and we'll need to do it quickly, so just for the record, confirm to me that you went to Orla Smith's between ten and eleven yesterday morning. You did whatever and then you left.'

'You can make it sound a little bit less sordid than that.'

'It is sordid,' said Macleod. 'You've got a family and a wife and you're doing it behind her back. I'm not sorry you got caught. I'm sorry you're wasting our time.'

'Well, can you just get hold of her and do it quiet, please? If you can talk to her and she confirms it, I could be out of here. Tell Mandy it was all a big mistake. Tell Mandy that, well, you know, you guys picked up the wrong person; you didn't understand where I was coming from.'

'She'll know though,' said Hope.

'Knowing is one thing, proof is another,' said O'Reilly. 'I thought you guys of all people would recognise that.'

Hope grunted, stood and marched out of the room. Macleod stood and followed her. She kept a distance from him as she marched off, pulling out her mobile phone from her pocket. She rang a number and Clarissa answered.

'Have you got anywhere?' started Clarissa.

'It's not him. He's been seeing Orla Smith. I need you to go to Orla Smith and confirm this. Then I'll let him out and we'll get back to looking at this case again.'

'Okay,' said Clarissa, 'you got an address? I'll take it it's somewhere near the CCTV camera.'

'Check-in with Ross. Ross will have all the details as ever,' said Hope and closed the phone call. By now Macleod had caught up with her.

'When did you know?' she raged. 'I sat in there with you asking questions of him. When did you know?'

'I thought you were never going to get there,' said Macleod. 'First time I saw them at the board together, it was pretty obvious. Don't be grumpy about it,' said Macleod suddenly. 'It's what I'm good at. It's my skill. You have skills too. I got to use mine; you will get to use yours. It doesn't matter who in the team pulls it out, that thread, the one that either leads to the unravelling of the mystery or to a dead end. Doesn't matter. If you're going up to Inspector, you've got to drop that ego.'

'I don't have an ego.'

'Of course, you have an ego,' said Macleod. 'You always had that pride that I can do this, I can do that. I don't need someone else. An ego's good, can help you, can drive you, but when you're up at the level you're going to and running a team, you got to lose it because it'll trip you up.'

'Well, thank you,' said Hope. 'I'll let you get back to your roster.' Macleod walked away, then suddenly turned around and stuck his tongue out at her. It dawned on her he was just happy to be back in an interview room.

There was no way he would stay a DCI, she thought. *He just doesn't like it. He just doesn't want to be there. Why on earth was he doing it?* And then it hit her. Because if he didn't, she would have to go elsewhere. Some days she could strangle the man, but other days . . . other days, he was tolerable.

Chapter 13

Clarissa Urquhart raced down in the small green car towards Orla Smith's house. She didn't like to run errands like this. She knew Macleod and Hope were waiting for her to bring in the other side of an affair so they could confirm its existence and they'd end up back at square one. Or, if they were having an affair, maybe they were covering for each other. No doubt the boss would find out.

Although things were being run slightly different now with the boss seemingly more aloof. Normally he'd be all over his people, insisting on reports back, opinions, thoughts, but it was Hope picking up everything, and in truth, it was different. Hope was more inclined towards the procedure. Macleod could deviate. He got an idea in his head, and he pushed you on it. At times you were speaking to him, and you got the impression he wasn't even listening, which frustrated Clarissa, but other times he was brilliant.

Hope didn't work that way. She was thorough. She got on top of things. She pushed, but Macleod seemed to have an outside-the-box ability, and Clarissa wondered if Hope sometimes got annoyed by it. She also knew the woman was under pressure. After all, there was talk of her going for the

DI position, but the force could be unfair. Would they judge her by the way this case was run, whether or not she solved it?

It was one thing being a sergeant, but you could always pass the buck up to the DI. On a lot of cases, the DI was the one leading the investigation. Hope had never truly done that. Well, at least not without some other circumstance pulling Macleod out of the way, and she wouldn't want to let him down. That was the other thing about Hope; she was loyal, almost to a fault, Clarissa thought. Hope would beat herself up if she didn't get to the bottom of this, if she couldn't do it before Macleod stepped in.

But none of that was Clarissa's concern. Instead, Ross and she would just have to get on with it. Their position hadn't changed. What they were doing, it may do. Ross may look at a move up to sergeant, and if he did that, well then, what about Clarissa? *Clarissa will just sit there and just get on with her job*, she told herself. *After all, it won't be that long until I'm out.*

Clarissa was older than Macleod. Not by a lot, but she was older, and she had seen him think about retirement before. She wasn't sure what she would do. No children, no partner, and getting to a stage in her life when having that someone to spend the last days of it with seemed like a good idea. The detective life didn't give you a lot of opportunities to socialise. Yes, when she was working in the art side, she got invited along to a lot more gallery openings and grander events, but they weren't real friends.

Being back at the golf club had made her think about when she played and about the friends she had made there. She needed to build a life for herself and soon. Her mind drifted to the head groundsman. *There had been that fireman down in Mull*, she thought, but she hadn't followed it up. Maybe she should follow this one up. Maybe she should make an effort this time.

Her driving had been on autopilot, and she only brought herself back to the present when she pulled the car up. She had that ability just to drive, mind elsewhere, but not the senses. If something had happened, if some car had pulled out in front of her, if something was going wrong, her brain would've kicked in. She could run fully on automatic. The only problem was sometimes you ended up miles away from where you were meant to be, but not this time.

Clarissa stepped out of the green car, closed the door, and strolled in her boots and shawl up to the house of Orla Smith. It was quaint and cottage-like, and she passed through an archway of leaves. Clarissa had thought about settling down somewhere like this. It was a part of the world she liked, for the North of Scotland was her home. That was where she was from. It was what she was.

She stopped for a moment, using her hands to trace the arch above her before looking at the stone path up to the wooden front door. There was a large black knocker on it. As she approached, she grabbed it and thundered on the door. She was never subtle.

'Orla Smith. Miss Orla Smith, this is Detective Sergeant Clarissa Urquhart. Are you in?'

Clarissa stood back from the door but heard nothing. She began to walk around the side, looking in through windows, but there were no lights on. She approached the rear door and found it open. She stepped inside.

'Orla Smith, this is Detective Sergeant Urquhart. Are you there? Orla Smith.'

Clarissa didn't like barging into people's houses, despite her rank, and slowly made her way across the kitchen, continuing to shout. She found a hallway and shouted upstairs. There could only have been about two rooms up there, given the size of the building. There came no reply. Clarissa decided to walk through the entire house.

She was right about upstairs, there were only two rooms, and one was a small bedroom, albeit quaint in its own way. Once again, she could see herself somewhere like this.

"Hello?'

A few paintings on the wall wouldn't have gone amiss. She'd have to get a few of the better ones. It'd been a while since she sat down properly and just enjoyed a good painting. Sit and stare, think about it, let it touch the senses. Exercise her imagination, a side she so often had to shut down in her current line of work.

Clarissa made her way back downstairs, and having thoroughly searched the house, stepped out of the back door again. There was a small wooden garage at the side, and Clarissa entered by a side door that was unlocked. Inside was a rather small metro, quite old, but easy to see out of, thought Clarissa. If you wanted something simple to drive, this was the car.

She walked back outside, exited the property, and strolled along to the next-door neighbours' property. This garden was not so well kept, and she could see an overturned trolley down one side. As she approached the door, there was no knocker, no number, and only a dirty glass pane that she couldn't see through. The walls of this cottage were beginning to peel. Clarissa wondered if anybody lived here. Regardless, she thundered on the door with her fist and stood back until the door opened abruptly. On the other side of it was a wary youth, possibly in his twenties. Beyond him, in the hallway, lurked a young woman.

"Excuse the intrusion,' said Clarissa. 'Detective Sergeant Clarissa Urquhart. I'm trying to contact Orla Smith next door. You wouldn't know where she is, would you?'

"That woman next door? To be honest," said the man, 'don't usually have many dealings with her.'

'That's understood, Mr . . .' Clarissa left the question hanging.

'McClintock. Ewan McClintock.'

'The person behind you is?'

'Shauna McClintock. This is our house. We haven't been in here long.' Suddenly a head appeared beside the man with long brown mousey hair on a woman that stood only four foot tall.

'Hello,' said Clarissa. 'You must be Shauna. Well, Mrs McClintock, Mr McClintock, please think, is there anything about Orla Smith at this time of day, at this time of the week that sticks out to you?'

'Only been here two months,' said Mr McClintock.

'Oh, Alan, but you don't do anything anyway. You're so busy working upstairs. He's a gamer. He helps design computer games,' said Shauna. 'Some days he's up there all day. I like to do a bit of work in the garden.'

Clarissa did her best not to turn her head and look, because having seen the state of it on the way in, she was trying to identify the piece of garden that got any attention.

'Orla tends to go out this time of the day, returns sometime. Depends on if her friend is . . .'

'Her friend?' asked Clarissa.

'Yes. There's a man who comes around occasionally. He never parks here. He always walks in. Anytime you talk to her afterwards, she's quite excited. Quite breathless too. You never see Mrs Smith out in a dressing gown or that, except when he's been round. Sometimes she walks out to the fence. She's got a dressing gown on like she's come out of the shower. Except, well, I'm not sure if she's come from the shower.'

'That's not what you told me. You didn't say shower. You said they'd been at it.'

'You mean he comes around for sex,' said Clarissa.

'Well, yes, if you want to put it that way.'

'If I showed you a photograph, would you be able to tell me if it's the man or not?'

'Of course,' said Shauna.

Clarissa pulled out her phone and started going through photographs. When she found the correct one, she showed it to Shauna. Alan bent down and looked as well. 'Yes,' they both said, 'that's him.'

'Tried to talk to him once,' said Alan. 'Blanked me. Just raced to get out of here.'

'It's probably because he's not meant to be here. His wife wouldn't be very happy,' said Clarissa. 'More importantly, do you know where Orla is? Her car's there.'

'She told me once,' said Shauna, 'that she goes walking, and yes, she does disappear out. She'll go up to the golf club. She's very into it. Always talks to me about the golf club if we ever catch up. That's not that often.'

'Do you know how she walks up to it?'

'Well,' said Shauna, 'if you go from here, take a left from the front of ours, keep walking and take a right. Then you'll see a gap in the wall. It's not a proper gap, it's not a proper path, but if you go through that bit and keep walking, you'll join one of the paths up to the club. Once you're there, you're basically on

123

the golf club estate, I would say. Keep walking straight from there. I think that's what she does. Follows that big circle around, brings you back to the same point and then you can come back again. Takes you a good hour to walk it.'

'Thank you,' said Clarissa and took out one of her cards, handing it to Shauna. 'If in the next hour, you see her come back, ring me, please.'

Shauna nodded, and as Clarissa turned away, she asked.

'Is she in trouble?'

'Not yet,' said Clarissa. 'We just need to find her to help someone else who is in trouble.'

Clarissa turned away, hearing the door shut behind her. As she exited the garden, she continued to look for that spot of grass, that bit of garden that got the attention of Shauna. It eluded her.

Clarissa didn't like the idea of having to walk the golf course, but at this point in time, there wasn't any other option, because she couldn't take the car to these paths. When she got back to her car, she opened the side door, adjusted her boots, happy they'd be good for walking in. She looked at the sky above, wondering if she'd get any rain, but in truth, the clouds were low and grey. With how chilly it was, they were more likely to get snow.

Clarissa followed the instructions given to her and soon reached the gap in the wall that had been described by Shauna. There was a bit of a climb up to it, but Clarissa managed, pushed through the small gap, and then walked a good two hundred metres in a heavily overgrown bit of vegetation. Tree branches cut this way and that, and she had to bend down several times. Each time, her knees complained at her.

Once she reached the firm path, Clarissa marched off,

deciding that she could go left or right, but it would come back to the same place. Taking the left, she suddenly felt good.

The arts team had been her work for so long in the police force, but Clarissa liked the outdoors. She was a Scot after all, and a highland Scot. Nothing would bring Clarissa more joy than marching along through a highland estate, or along a forest, wrapped up in her large shawl. She always felt warm and ready to go, and this time was no exception.

As she walked, she scanned around her. When the path first broke the trees, she found herself alongside one of the holes. She had no idea which it was, but obviously, it was on the parkland course. From here, they were a reasonable distance from the sea and she could hear some of the birds and the crunch of the gravel as she walked along the path. The golf course felt eerily silent with the membership not being allowed to play.

As she marched along, Clarissa thought about retirement. She thought about coming out to the golf course, out with the girls, playing a round, and then in for either a hot pot of tea and a large baguette or sandwich, or maybe even a couple of whiskys. Maybe she would leave the green sports car at home, taking a taxi. It wasn't often she got to go out like this, striding along, happy as Larry and enjoying the sounds of nature around her. She only missed the whack of the odd golf ball, but inside, she was in her happy place.

As Clarissa reached the top of the path and it turned down a hill back into woodland, she was able to look across and see one of the tee boxes. Clarissa wasn't sure which hole it was, but what she could see was someone was on the tee box. That was unusual. Nobody was meant to be there.

She decided to take a brief look, but started to get a cold chill as she drew nearer. There was a figure there, but there was also a golf bag. The figure wasn't moving, and it didn't look like it was doing anything inside the golf bag, rather it was lying over the top of it. When she got closer, the chill became very real.

Clarissa began to run towards the figure. Arriving, she touched the side of the neck, encouraging the figure to wake up. 'Orla, Orla, this is Sergeant Urquhart. Wake up for me. Are you okay?'

As Clarissa tried to grab the shoulders and shake the figure, the golf bag collapsed and Orla Smith fell to the ground, landing face down, but then spinning over onto her back. Clarissa followed her down, touching the side of the neck, listening to the mouth, and then realised that there wasn't a lot of movement. Stepping back, however, she saw that Orla Smith had been cut across the chest and also the neck had been punctured. It wasn't a slash. It was a push-in knife wound, but it looked like it might have been as deadly as the one suffered by Sandy Mackintosh.

Clarissa pulled out her mobile phone from under her shawl, dialled 999 and requested an ambulance to the golf course. She looked around. There was nobody else here. She picked up the phone again, dialled, and then heard Ross at the other end. She almost gave a sigh of relief.

'Als, I'm on the,' she looked over the little wooden markers on the other side of the tee box, 'the thirteenth hole on the parkland with Orla Smith. I'm about to go to work on her. I think she's dead. Thirteenth. I've ordered an ambulance. Get down here!'

She put the phone down beside her, turned, and started to work on Orla Smith, but as she did so, Clarissa knew that the second victim was already gone.

Chapter 14

Macleod looked up from his rather large desk and saw Hope approaching. He was still getting used to it because his old one back downstairs was much smaller, but then he didn't have so many papers to shove around. Now it seemed that the desk was constantly flanked by piles that needed to be worked through. He'd also had to get into the habit of locking the office door each time he went out because of some of the confidential material inside. He popped up some time ago, telling Hope to come and get him when they needed to go back in to talk to Padraig O'Reilly, but as he looked up at Hope, he got the feeling that he wasn't about to be leaving his office anytime soon.

'Orla Smith's dead, Seoras.'

'What?' blurted Macleod in surprise. 'She's dead?'

'May have gone for a walk from the house, was found on the thirteenth hole of the parkland course, over the top of a golf bag. Clarissa tried to help her, but looks like she was dead before Clarissa got there.'

Macleod nodded, instantly turning away, and giving that impression that his brain had gone into full gear.

'So, what do you make of that?' asked Hope.

'What do I make of it? What do you think?'

'She's a funny one to take out. She never really talked that much about her position, although she was probably anti-the-tour deal.'

'If that's what it's about; remember, she was having an affair. You'd better check on the whereabouts of O'Reilly's wife, just in case she's got wind of it.'

'Of course, I will do. But the way that her corpse was set up at the golf course?'

'Yes,' said Macleod. 'Except that she's not a golfer, never has been. She looks after the staff. The tableau with Mackintosh playing the hole, fits him. This just seems . . .'

'I was thinking the same,' said Hope.

'You got anything else?'

'Well, I have Ross looking into the usual. He's checking the CCTV cameras again of that area. Should be coming back to me shortly.'

'Do you know where anybody else was at the time? Obviously, it wasn't Pádraig. He's downstairs still, I take it?'

'I'll just let him go. He's quite upset at the moment.'

'I'm not surprised. It was good he was with us though. As long as, well, the body was fresh enough,' mused Macleod.

'Jona gave an initial estimate that the body had only been dead for a couple of hours, so yes. Pádraig O'Reilly is definitely off the hook for this one.'

'What do you know about her though?' asked Macleod to Hope.

'Well, that's the thing. There's not much to her. She has this affair going on, but outside of the golf club, and Clarissa says her little house doesn't appear to be much. Clarissa said the garden was done up so well, and it would take somebody

129

most of their days to keep it that way. Maybe she was a bit of excitement for Mr O'Reilly. Maybe he knew she wouldn't be one to want to run off and broadcast it.'

'Well, if he can tell that,' said Macleod, 'he's a better man than me.'

'You've never been in an affair?'

'No,' said Macleod quickly, 'but to be honest, I think you ladies are always the harder ones to judge.'

'Greater depth,' said Hope, 'can understand that. Or more unstable.'

'One or the other,' said Macleod, and Hope saw him give a cheeky grin when she looked at him. 'Either way, how did she die?'

'Slashed across the chest and punctured throat.'

'Punctured?'

'Yes, punctured. Knife driven in, not slit.'

'Now that is interesting,' said Macleod.

'Glad you think so,' said Hope, and then reached for her pocket. Macleod could hear it vibrating.

'Ross,' said Hope to the phone. 'What do we know?' Macleod watched as she nodded several times. 'And you are doing what at the moment?'

Again, there was silence as Hope listened in on the phone. When she closed down the call, she turned back to Macleod. 'Ross says that the CCTV is only showing up two people passing by the area. One's Amy Johnson. She's been identified as being up at the club as well. The other one's Cecil Ayers. We may need to go and talk to them both, but it looks like Johnson was seen about.'

'Are you wanting me with you?' asked Macleod.

'Ross is busy. So's Clarissa, tidying up the other end. I need somebody. Besides, you look like you need a break from all this paperwork.'

'I don't need a break from it. I need it setting fire to,' said Macleod, standing up and walking over to get his coat. As he did so, the side door of his office opened, and his secretary walked in.

'Do you need me, Linda? I'm just going out.'

'I just wanted to put these other reports on your desk. Where would you like them, Inspector?'

'Name's Seoras. Don't you start with that Inspector stuff as well. Bung them on the desk somewhere. I'm not sure how long I'll be, so you can hold the calls. If it's the Assistant Chief Constable, tell him to contact my mobile.'

The woman nodded as Macleod made for the door before opening it and letting Hope walk out first.

Over her shoulder, she heard Macleod say, 'Did the coffee arrive, by the way?' There was a loud tut when the response came in the negative.

The pair of them took their own cars up to the golf club in case Macleod would have to disappear. On arrival, they were greeted by Sergeant Halford.

'What's happening, Sergeant?' asked Hope.

'I've got Mr Ayers inside, along with Miss Johnson. A couple of others have turned up from the board. I've had some constables taking down where they've been, just filling in their whereabouts. At the moment, Jona is out with her team on the thirteenth. I believe Clarissa is still with her. Ross is running around picking other things up as well. He was checking through CCTV of here and of the roads.'

'Excellent. I think we'll go and talk to Cecil Ayers.'

'I'd stop by Ross on the way,' said Macleod.

'Of course.' She turned to walk down to the club, hearing Halford give a quick word to the Inspector behind her. That was the thing about Macleod. Despite the fact everyone was on first-name terms or meant to be, so many of them still called him Inspector.

It felt like Hope was taking his job, felt like she was filling his shoes as opposed to Hope running the case. She didn't like that. She didn't like the awe he was held in. Although, to be fair, the man had none of it. She did laugh when he talked to some of the constables, though, and she saw them jump.

The pair found Ross running around the incident room within the golf club, as ever, thoroughly efficient, and busy.

'Oh, glad you're here, Sergeant,' said Ross. 'CCTV. Cars of Cecil Ayers and Amy Johnson are there. I've also been going through the CCTV of the club. Cecil Ayers certainly came in, but that's after the murder took place. Amy Johnson is in before. I have no actual footage of her at the time, but she is seen probably about a half hour, an hour afterwards, up here. Everybody else I cannot find in the area. I believe their statements have said they weren't. Not that that precludes them from being out there.'

'Only Padraig O'Reilly,' said Macleod. 'He was with us.'

Ross nodded and quickly turned back to doing his work, before turning round over his shoulder and saying, 'Have you had coffee yet?'

Hope noticed he was talking to Seoras.

'I'll sort it,' said Macleod. 'Get back to whatever you're doing.' Ross went to protest, but Hope shot him a look. She let Macleod disappear off to get the coffee. Five minutes later, they were sitting with Cecil Ayers, who was at the bar and by the looks of it, had drunk about four whiskies.

'The thing is,' said Cecil, 'she was a good one. Orla Smith ran this place. She was on top of the staff. Before, it was a joke. Yet she had no clue about golf.' Hope saw the man was nearly falling off his chair, but she was keen to hear him talk.

'Came up here afterwards, found out when I came in. Can't believe it,' said Cecil. 'Two of them. Two of them, draped over a golf bag. She never used a golf bag in her life.'

'Is there anyone that would have—how shall I put this?' said Hope. 'Had a grudge against Orla.'

'Orla? No. O'Reilly? Yes. He's all spit and feathers. Orla? Quiet, efficient, always get everything done. Nothing ever a problem. Everybody liked Orla.'

'Everybody?' queried Macleod. 'Are you sure everybody?'

'Well,' said Cecil, 'somebody didn't, but the board, we were very happy. She did a lot of that side of the work for us. Quiet. There's been no staff problems since she took over. She was somebody you would want; somebody you were keen to keep.'

'Where were you, Mr. Ayers?' asked Hope. 'We spotted you on the CCTV in the area. You would have been close to the paths that allowed access onto the golf course. However, your car stopped for a bit.'

'Yes,' he said. 'I did stop for a bit. If you drive along the road coming up to the course, you take a left about a half a mile out. There's a little car park. You can look out to the Moray Firth. I was there. I was there thinking about Sandy.'

'Why there?' asked Hope.

'Because it's not a very well-used car park,' said Cecil. 'If I came up here, I would be right in this seat if I thought about Sandy. I'm right here because I'm thinking about Orla. All I want is for that man behind the bar to keep giving me stuff so I can forget what's happened to . . . It's rubbish,' said Cecil

133

suddenly.

'You know, we used to have the one course and it was great. Everybody got behind it. Now, what do we have? What is this that causes all these problems? Meant to be about golf, meant to be about family and friends and having a good time. It's not meant to be about big money. Orla wasn't about big money. Orla was just, well, get things done nice and quietly, be efficient, so good you didn't even notice her. That's how good she was. When she wanted something done with the staff, she didn't stand up and make a big point about it. She had everybody convinced before they even walked into the room to vote on it. She understood what she was doing.'

'But with regards to the decision coming up?'

'She would have gone with whatever Padraig voted. When it came to the golf thing, she voted however Padraig voted. Sometimes I think there was something more than just a working relationship between the two of them.'

'What makes you say that?' asked Hope.

'The way she looked at him. The way she was around him. Oh, she liked him.'

Cecil began to cough badly, throwing up large chunks of phlegm into his mouth, which he dispatched into a large handkerchief. He then drank another neat shot of whisky. Hope looked at the man. Could this be a killer? Maybe he was drinking so much because of what he'd just done.

'We'll come back to you if we need any more, Mr Ayers,' said Hope. She took Macleod back into the incident room office.

'What do you think?' she asked.

'What do you think?' retorted Macleod.

'We can't trace where he was. He's now getting sozzled, possibly after having done something, but then again, he didn't after the first one if it's him.'

'Anything else?'

'I've got you here to be my help, not to be ticking off the boxes like I'm going through an exam.'

'You're always going through an exam—that's the point,' said Macleod suddenly. 'You need to be ticking off the boxes. You need to be sitting asking what about this? What about that?'

'What box are you thinking about in particular?' said Hope testily.

'Physical strength,' said Macleod. 'There's no way that man legs it out to the thirteenth and back. Physically, Orla Smith would have a chance against him. She didn't look a weak woman and Clarissa mention her good looking garden. She'd have strong muscles doing that. She was only in her fifties,' said Macleod. 'I've got a problem seeing how that guy overpowers and kills her. I also have a problem seeing how he takes on Sandy Macintosh. Granted, it would probably be the most disappointing fight I've ever watched, but to operate a blade as well? Not for me,' said Macleod.

'What about Amy Johnson?' Hope said. 'She was up here.'

'But Amy Johnson wasn't around for the first one,' said Macleod.

'Doesn't mean she can't be around for the second one.'

'No,' said Macleod. 'It doesn't. How about a sweep of the locker room?'

'Already had Ross onto it.'

'Including the ladies'?'

'Including the ladies'.'

'What did they find?' asked Macleod.

'Nothing,' said Hope.

'Have you had a look yourself?' Macleod asked.

135

'No, I was down with you, wasn't I? Wasn't up here.'

'Well, I'd have a look yourself,' said Macleod. 'Always cover off things like that when you haven't got any available information coming towards you.'

Hope tutted, but she marched off, with Macleod following her, and they went down to pass through the men's locker room. She asked a nearby constable whose locker was whose, and slowly they opened up the lockers of Andrew Peters, Cecil Ayers, Alastair Begley and Padraig O'Reilly. There seemed to be very little change in them from previous days, and then when they went through to the women's, Orla Smith's was empty, while Amy Johnson's seemed to have smelly gym kit in it.

'Nothing much, then,' said Hope.

'Nothing much,' said Macleod dryly behind her.

'Somebody's making a point, though,' said Hope.

'And you think it's to do with the vote?' said Macleod.

'You think it isn't?'

Macleod seemed to disappear for a minute, looking around him, and Hope watched as he chewed over his thoughts before he turned back to her and said, 'Dormie five. We had two for, four against. We're now two for and three against. Certainly, a possibility. Certainly, something to think about.'

'You think there's something else?'

'I don't know, Hope,' said Macleod. 'I really don't know.'

Chapter 15

'Will you still be requiring your room?' asked Alastair Begley, causing Hope to look up suddenly from her desk.

'Excuse me?'

'Will you still be requiring your room? Normally we use this one when we have votes.'

'And why would that bother you at the moment?' asked Hope.

'Because tonight's the vote.'

It had been over a day since the body of Orla Smith had been found on the thirteenth hole and despite constant interviewing, nothing new had come to light. Cecil Ayres was still in the frame, although Hope was seeing Macleod's point. The idea of this old man—firstly committing the murder and then hanging Orla over a golf bag and also, secondly, having what motive—was running through her head.

Amy Johnson was up at the club, but she'd been seen inside the clubhouse. Peters hadn't been anywhere near the golf course, or at least that's what he claimed, and his car hadn't been picked up on any CCTV. There just wasn't enough information. There were too few certainties, but that wasn't unusual at the start of a case. They weren't that long into it, albeit the idea that a second victim had been dispatched bothered Hope no end. It did point to the idea of the great vote for whether the tour could come to the club as being the main motive.

'What vote?' asked Hope.

'The election. We've got to have an election for a new Club Secretary. Somebody's got to fill Sandy's position. We're having it tonight. We usually use this room as an adjunct to the large hall down below. It's where we keep the candidates.'

'You're having a vote?' said Hope suddenly. 'You're seriously telling me you're going ahead with the vote? I thought you would've cancelled it. We've just had another person die. Does anybody want to stand?'

Hope realised she'd lost it. She was beginning to get that understanding of Macleod when he seemed to snap on occasions. *Were these people for real? Why on earth would you have a vote?*

'Yes, we're going ahead. I mean, it's important. You can't have a club without governance. The constitution says we have to instigate and get the vote going quickly, especially in the event of a death. If it's something longer-term, we can stretch it out more like if you're hiring someone onto the board, a bit like Amy.'

'You've got people dying.'

'You think there'll be more?' asked Alastair.

'You think there won't be? What leads you to the conclusion that this is it?' asked Hope.

'So, you think there will be?'

Hope stood up from behind her desk hoping that the increased height, given that she now towered above the man, would give her words somewhat more gravitas.

'People are dead. I don't know if there will be more murders or not because so far, we haven't identified who is committing them. We have an open mind, and we are investigating. It would seem to me to be very poor form to actually hold a vote given the current situation. Orla died a day ago.'

'I can understand you thinking it's cold and callous, but Orla would be for it as well. In fact, she was in the process of helping to organise this vote tonight. We were all agreed, the club has to go on. We can't let this opportunity go past. We need to vote on it. It sets a precedent, don't you think? What will we be? What will the club be? Are we this course, that course? Do we stand for tradition or not? It's important that that's settled.'

'You want to do this in the middle of everything that's going on? You've got two deaths. Pádraig O'Reilly was shown to be having an affair with Orla Smith, who then died. Now, we know Pádraig didn't do it because he was with us, but that won't stop the rumour mill; that won't stop everything else that's going on.'

'But it's important,' said Alastair.

Hope stared at him. 'I can't stop you having a vote,' said Hope. 'I can't stop the business of the club. I can stop the course being used because we're out there combing it and working on it. However, I think it's ill-advised and I would suggest you don't. If, however, you decide to continue, you may use downstairs but this room remains ours for this time. I'd appreciate it if you'd find a different room for your candidates.'

Hope watched as Alastair Begley suddenly bit his lip as if the decision wasn't really going to go down well with a lot of people.

'Okay,' he said, 'I'll see what I can do.'

'It's a room,' said Hope. 'Just find another room.'

'It's not just a room, it's tradition. It's what we do. It's the way we run things. I don't think you're getting that.'

'And I don't think you understand what's going on here. How can you be so obsessed with tradition amid the killings that have gone on?'

'It's what we are. We've been here as a club for so long, and yes, times at the moment are strange. I don't think we've had murders in the club before, but the processes and the way we do things have kept things running before. This is tradition. This is the very thing I'm standing for.'

'So, let me understand this,' said Hope. 'You don't want the tour to come here and take on the parkland course; you'd rather they didn't. If we don't get a vote done in time, the tour will probably clear off anyway, but instead, for tradition's sake, you're going to make sure there is a place for a vote. If somebody's getting rid of your people so they can stack the odds to make that vote, you do realise that you would be enabling them to do that. Instead, doing nothing would be an easier way to block it.'

'You can't stand for tradition and just willy-nilly manipulate things left and right. I have a duty to the membership. I have a duty to the course and to tradition and to golf.'

Hope stared in disbelief. 'You have your room downstairs. Please don't interfere with the running of our investigation. Thank you, Mr Begley.'

The man nodded, turned, and walked from the room and Hope thought he looked rather pale for all of how he wasn't budging. The events of the last few days must have been draining. He seemed to speak reasonably fondly of Sandy and

Orla. When you work with people, even if you weren't that close as friends, it did make a difference. When you worked together, you couldn't help but feel something.

She sat back down, put her feet up on the table and let out a long sigh. Things weren't moving at the moment. The killings are happening somewhere so open that it wouldn't be difficult for anyone to get there. They had several people involved. All these board members, well, five now after two being removed, maybe they weren't even the problem. She'd started Ross interviewing members of the club staff, but that seemed hopeless.

People who really understood the issues were on that board. If there was motive around the tour coming, it was there. If it wasn't, what was there to keep Sandy Mackintosh and Orla Smith together. As far as they'd investigated, there were no links between the two. They hadn't been anywhere together in the past. They didn't really do that much together on the board. Orla, according to Cecil Ayres, simply handled the staff. Sandy was more into the competitions and the events that the club would set up. Their only liaison had been to cater for those events, make sure that they happened. It wasn't a large crossover. The ideal candidate for Orla Smith would've been Pádraig O'Reilly, except they had held Pádraig when the murder happened.

Pádraig's wife was seen in her house by the neighbours; she hadn't left it. Hope didn't believe it was a crime of passion. The prevailing theory was a change of personnel to enable dormie five to happen and for the tour to come. If that was the case, tonight's vote would be critical. No one had come to Hope to say, 'Block the vote.' No one. Traditionalists.

Hope remained up in the appropriated office, running

through reports and taking a call from Jona. She'd pull everybody in tomorrow. They needed to sit down and go through it again. This is what Macleod did; when he hit a dead end, he pulled the team together. But not tonight. She picked up the phone and called Seoras. He was just on his way home.

'This is why you're doing it, isn't it?' she said. 'These better hours.'

'Jane's enjoying them,' he said, 'I don't know if that's enough though, to sit this side of the fence.'

'They're having a vote tonight, Seoras; they're trying to replace Sandy Mackintosh.'

'So, they're intending to replace everyone?'

'Can you believe it,' said Hope. 'Alastair Begley came in and practically begged me for the room downstairs and asked when we were clearing out so he could actually use the room I'm in at the moment. Well, I gave him a short shift on that, but they're going ahead with it. I mean, if you don't want this thing to happen, the easiest thing to do would be to block people going onto the board.'

'It would,' said Macleod. 'Having spoken to Dermot McKinley, the tour isn't going to hang about forever. What does bother me though is how many times can you kill someone. How many times can you hit the press and then not suffer the bad publicity from it? The tour won't want bad publicity. Somebody's playing a dangerous calculation if that's what's going on.'

'It is. I'm more and more convinced this is what it's about.'

'Keep a wide eye,' said Macleod suddenly. 'A wide eye, Hope. I know there's pressure on you and there shouldn't be, but don't force the resolution. You can't do that. You'll come to the wrong conclusion. Be careful.'

'I'm not inexperienced, Seoras.'

'And neither am I,' said Macleod suddenly, his voice raising. 'I don't give you this advice because I think you're immature. I don't give you it because I think you're some kind of Gung Ho western fighter. I give you it because I think it's needed, because I needed it in that position, and I still needed it after twenty years of doing the position.'

Hope took a deep breath. When he got something under his bonnet, he was going to tell you.

'Just be careful. Make sure everything fits in, all the killings, because if you're right, you're going to get more. You do realise that, don't you?'

'Of course,' said Hope. 'But more than that, tonight's meeting is actually important. If they don't get a candidate that wants the tour voted in, they're back to square one, and like you say, they can't just keep killing people.'

'How does it stand at the moment,' asked Macleod.

'Well, they've only got five members at the moment. They've got two for, and three against. One's heavily discredited due to his indiscretions around his family and Orla Smith, but he's not off the board yet.'

'No, he's not,' said Macleod, 'but watch out for that one. They might try and push him off. It might show you who is actually doing this.'

'I'd better go,' said Hope. 'I can hear them all in downstairs. I'll see you tomorrow when I pull the team in together. Can you get down here, Seoras?'

'What time do you want me?'

'Will ten be all right?'

'What time do you want me? Stop giving me a time when you think I'll actually be in the office and then able to get down

143

to you. I'll come direct. I told you, you've got me as an extra, so please treat me as one, not as the boss all the time.'

'Eight-thirty, see you here,' said Hope, 'and it's not good the way this is working. You understand that, don't you?'

'Of course, I do. If everything goes through and we both step up, you'll get extra bods. You'll need them.'

'Thanks, Seoras,' said Hope, and put the phone down. As she left the room, she met Clarissa Urquhart coming up the stairs, running towards the office. She seemed a little bit out of puff. She watched as Clarissa held her hand up, entered the room, and then came back out with a notepad and a pen.

'What are you doing?'

'I just want to take some notes, see what goes on.'

'Let's head down then,' said Hope. 'Is it a big crowd?'

'I think most of the membership is here, and I'm not surprised, are you? I mean, it's been a bit dramatic. Most of them will be out just to see what's going on.'

'How up-to-date are you with what's going on amongst the membership?' said Hope.

'What do you mean?' asked Clarissa.

'What's the sound amongst them? Are they for this tour? Are they against it? What's the biz with it?'

'The biz? Who's down with the kids, eh?'

'You know what I mean. You've been in a golf club before, you've been a golfer. Alastair Begley came up and told me this vote was going to go ahead tonight. Asked for our room. I don't get this, Clarissa, understand? Why would you keep going ahead? Why doesn't Begley just turn around and say, "We can't do anything at the moment; we've got dead people everywhere." Cancel the vote. Make it not happen and the tour clears off?'

'You don't get the tradition, do you? You don't get the idea of things being done properly.'

'Not when somebody else isn't doing it properly.'

'There's probably a romantic inside of Alastair Begley. He sees the golf, the institution of it. He sees that this is something good in the world that should be preserved, similar in the art world sometimes. I've seen people put art before straightforward matter-of-fact, preservation of life. People talk about paintings being stolen, where somebody's died as if the death is the irrelevant bit, what happened to the painting is the important one. As much as I love my paintings, as much as I love my art,' said Clarissa, 'human life is at the forefront of it; it's the most important thing. Unfortunately, some people seem to cheapen it for what needs to be done.'

'Well, what's the feeling on the floor tonight?' asked Hope. 'I get what you're saying, but what's going to happen?'

'I was talking to the head groundsman, Frank Macleod. He gets to hear a lot of things, talks to a lot of people, and he's proving to be quite a good source,' said Clarissa. 'Not a bad looker with it.' She gave Hope a wink. Hope gave a faint smile. She wasn't really in the mood for that sort of thing, but it was Clarissa. You had to let her be Clarissa.

'They had thought that Marion Linwood would be the one to step in. A lot of the members like her, but she's also very inexperienced. John Durbin's been around the club longer. He's seen as a safe pair of hands by people, but he's very pro getting the tour in. Marion would be anti. I also think there's been a highlighting of the issues between the two courses. You see, the thing about the tour is a lot of the ordinary members won't understand the downsides to that event coming in. It's quite hard sometimes to explain. They see the bright lights;

they see the glamour.

'Everything in life comes with a cost,' said Clarissa, 'but too often, we don't even look at what that cost is, just what the benefit would be. Durbin will win tonight,' she said. 'It won't be by a mile because it's been hard to overturn Marion's popularity. Like I say, she's really well-liked, Frank reckons. Maybe three-fifths of the vote to Durbin, but it'll be enough.'

The pair went downstairs and stood at the back watching as statements were made by John Durbin and Marion Linwood. The whole process was extremely formal with Alastair Begley running most of it. Peters, however, was there to stand up and administer the final vote as the room split towards two different bins for votes to be placed into. It took only fifteen minutes after that for the vote to be counted and for Andrew Peters to stand up with Cecil Ayres and announce that John Durbin would be the next Club Secretary. Hope stared across the room at Alastair Begley as the result was announced. His face was red. For a gaunt man, he seemed to be full of colour.

She wondered if he wanted to storm out, but as he'd set up the proceedings, he had to make sure everything was cleared away afterwards. Standing at the side of the hall as the room was returned to its original state, Hope noted that Amy Johnson kept out of the limelight. She was even dressed in beige trousers and a jumper. She had no vote herself and she seemed to speak to very few people apart from one young man who came up, clearly believing that she might respond to some advances. She brushed him off, not impolitely, but firmly. As she went to leave the room, Hope intercepted her.

'You must be happy,' said Hope. 'Vote going your way. That's three on your side, only another two and you can get your tour to come.'

The woman smiled. Hope saw the red lipstick, not over the top, but certainly something a man would notice.

'It's sad, but you're absolutely right. None of us would want Sandy Mackintosh out of the way,' said Amy. 'Sandy loved this club, but John will do a good job for it—that's what everyone says. And we can't vote anyway. We need another member.'

'I assume that's going to happen quickly.'

'Not my rules,' said Amy. 'It's what is in the club constitution, but I'd expect it within a week, maybe even quicker depending on what happens. There'll be a board meeting soon to talk about it. In fact, it's the most important business we have to attend to. We don't vote on things unless we can go dormie—dormie five. It's quite a quaint term, isn't it?' said Amy.

'You're lucky you've got your alibi,' said Hope. 'Otherwise, you'd have been a prime suspect. You realise that, don't you?'

'Very much, Detective. Very much, but I'm just doing my job.'

Hope watched the woman go and then turned back to Alastair Begley, Peters, and Cecil Ayres talking in the corner. Pádraig O'Reilly was also lurking, but clearly, the man had been keeping out of sight during the evening, for Hope hadn't seen him in the room. She watched as a round of whisky was brought down and the four of them drank a shot together. Hope heard the names of Sandy Mackintosh and Orla Smith being mentioned, but all she could think was, there were at least three men standing there who were surely in the firing line.

Chapter 16

Hope had made it home that night for approximately five hours of sleep. John had returned from his conference and she was fighting that battle of being so pleased to see him that she didn't want to go to sleep and knowing that the job required her to get some shut-eye. She couldn't think correctly; she couldn't operate properly if she simply didn't sleep. Even Macleod had to sleep sometimes.

She felt that the three hours she got was good sleep, and the other two spent with John probably did her the world of good. She was able to talk to him, not about the specifics of the case, but about her, about how she was feeling. She didn't want to do that to anyone else. The team couldn't understand; it wasn't their burden to carry. She didn't want to tell Seoras. John said she was daft, but it was always a thing with her. She knew Macleod thought of her in a good light, knew that he trusted her. After all, he was the one recommending that she step up. She also didn't want to disappoint him. John tried to explain that issues were not disappointing; they were just issues. The man would understand.

Hope never understood what her confidence thing was around Macleod. Maybe it was because on occasion she felt like he didn't think she was ready. He did now; he'd said so. He'd put the wheels in motion without hesitation. He didn't want Clarissa to step up. No. Detective Inspector Clarissa Urquhart was a terrifying thought. A Rottweiler on the loose. She had laughed at that one, and John hadn't quite understood.

Now she was awaiting a coffee from Ross with the time barely reaching half past eight. Macleod wasn't here yet. The rest of the team were gathering. Jona had just arrived, and the diminutive Asian woman approached her. Hope had that situation they always had, the height difference being so significant. Generally, Hope tried to sit down when Jona was about. Grab a perch on the edge of a desk. Something that would make the height difference look less. But Hope was at the front now about to coordinate proceedings as Jona came up to her, her face a little bit anxious.

'You got everything you need?' said Hope. 'I'll be letting you take the reins in a bit.'

'I'm fine with that. How are you?'

'I'm okay. I think I got sleep last night. John's back.' Jona gave out a broad smile. 'Not like that,' said Hope. 'At least not all like that. It was good.'

'I've been worried about you,' said Jona. 'Everybody needs that person. You forget that. Macleod has always had Jane.'

'What about you?' asked Hope.

'Well, that would be telling,' she said. 'Look at them. Ross has got his Angus, and Clarissa . . . well, I think she's looking for someone.'

'Well, it's going to have to be a heck of a man,' said Hope, causing Jona to laugh. 'Come on, we'd better get down to work. The boss is a bit tardy.'

'We've got another thirty seconds,' said Jona. 'He'll be here.

He's not going to abuse that sort of thing. Macleod will be here. He expects everyone else to keep good time.'

As if by magic, Hope heard Ross shouting across the room, 'Morning, sir.'

'Morning, Ross,' said Macleod. He looked very refreshed. Much more than Hope.

'Morning, Seoras. Glad you could be here.'

'At your disposal, as I said.' He took up a seat to the side, letting Jona continue her conversation with Hope. Hope waited, letting Jona talk for another minute or two, until Ross had dispensed coffees to everyone, at which point she gave a nod to Clarissa to close the door.

'Right,' said Hope. 'Good job so far but we need to get onto this. We need to know exactly what's going on. We're going to go over our main players. Jona's going to start by taking us through this latest killing, now we've got the full details back from forensics.'

'Thanks,' said Jona, and stood up looking around at the team, and a couple of other constables who had joined them, as well as Sergeant Halford.

'First thing to note,' said Jona, 'is the second murder is a distinctly different killing. The knife used was broader, not so expertly wielded. When the neck was attacked, it was punctured, not slit. The cuts across the chest, not so accurate and deep. The body was also propped up in a different fashion. Sandy Mackintosh was held up by the golf club. It took a bit of work. The artistry, if I can say that, was good. There was almost a care in it. It was made to have Sandy look like he was hitting a shot on the fifteenth.'

'Artistry?' said Hope.

'Yes,' said Jona. 'It was like somebody cared. They didn't just kill him, they set him up as a montage. Some sort of emblem.'

'If you just killed somebody, why do you want to make them an emblem . . . unless you're going to mock them?' queried Hope.

'I disagree,' said Clarissa. 'You don't always kill somebody because you're angry with them. Sometimes it has to be done.'

Hope saw Macleod raise his eyebrow at Clarissa. 'Not the best description of that feeling,' said Macleod.

'You know what I mean, Seoras,' said Clarissa. 'Don't be so picky. Sometimes it's business, isn't it? Sometimes it's a dead end, and an old friend gets in the way. Sometimes, you just have to do it. It's like those mafia films, isn't it? 'Oh, go and take so and so out. Oh, by the way, shoot them in the back of the head, and don't let them see it's coming.' As if it's some sort of favour. That's the way they get, isn't it? It's like a default setting in their head.'

'Absolutely,' said Jona. 'It's like a displaced feeling. It gets put to the secondary instead of the primary where it should exist, but it's still there.'

'The second killing, not so?' said Hope.

'No. She's propped up in a haphazard fashion, just lying over the golf bag. The tableau set up is not as detailed, like it was copied rather than coming from personal knowledge. Orla Smith was half dumped. The other thing is, Orla Smith is not a golfer.'

'That is right,' said Clarissa; 'she's not a golfer. She organises staff. He should have propped her up with a clipboard.'

'That's pretty disrespectful,' said Ross.

'No, it's not,' said Clarissa. 'It's making a point, and it's making a very valid point. Look, Als, how would you prop the rest of us up? I'd prop you up over a computer. I'd prop Hope up, probably over a car, running around outside—some sort of action montage. As for Seoras, he'd be in that seat looking out the window.'

'Hopefully, nobody is looking to prop me up anywhere,' said Macleod quite sternly. 'I think your point's made, before we get a little too carried away.'

'She's right,' said Hope. 'Anything else from the surrounding land, Jona?'

'Nothing. We're still combing, trying to find . . . we haven't found either knife. That's the other thing to be aware of. The first knife, we're looking for a much thinner blade. I'm still trying to identify it, but I think if we do, it's going to open up the idea of what was going on, on that first killing. The second killing, well, it's more butchery than actual killing.

'Also, the golf bag was stolen from outside the clubhouse. The owner was inside having lunch and didn't realise until he went to collect it after this had all kicked off. The clubs and other items from the bag were dumped in a nearby bush.'

'Thank you, Jona,' said Hope. 'Let's get back to the purpose of the killings. Why have they been happening?'

'The vote,' said Clarissa. 'It's the vote, isn't it? Somebody's trying to get the vote through. It's this dormie five thing. But I think you said to me last night, the traditionalists are getting in their own way. They could just stop this so easily.'

'Is it the vote?' asked Macleod suddenly.

'What else is it, Seoras?' said Clarissa.

'Seoras is right,' said Hope. 'We've got to be careful. Too often, we get sold ideas about what's happening.'

'The thing is,' said Ross, 'the vote obviously isn't very public knowledge.'

'Some people in the club know about it,' replied Clarissa.

'Frank, the head gardener knows about it. The ground staff talk about it. The membership, as I spoke to them, aren't overly aware of it, except they do know that the tour is coming, but they don't understand the full detail. They don't understand the implications for either course, and it's not being made aware to them.'

'Why not?' asked Jona. 'Why are they not telling everybody?'

'It's board business,' said Clarissa. 'You've got to understand that the board deal with certain aspects. They don't tell everything that they do. They'll hold it back. They'll have their reasons. There's a confidentiality, in that members need to know things when they need to know them. Not at this stage, there's no done deal. What are you going to do, get the people to vote on whether or not they want the tour to be here? Most golfers would jump up and down. All the extra bits of what happens afterwards, what happens with the money, what money comes, what they have to do to prepare, most golfers are not aware of this, and they'll struggle to appreciate it. All they'll see is the tour. Let's bring it here!'

'Do we have any other motives?' asked Hope. 'Ross, run us through the people again. What have we got on them?'

'Well,' said Ross, 'Chairman Andrew Peters: re-enactment enthusiast, particular interest in Spain. I haven't got much else beyond that. He's just a typical businessman. He's retired; made his money in what seems legitimate sales through pots and pans. I'm struggling to dig up anything on him. Not even a parking ticket.

'Cecil Ayers: always been a golfer, a councillor with a fairly clean record, a bit insipid when it comes to voting. No major issues, kept out of it. He seemed to enjoy the perks that came with being a councillor. Most of the people in the area that he served report him as being reasonably decent. Not a star but not bad either.

'Amy Johnson,' said Ross, 'seems to be quite intense about her work. I can't find her doing anything much outside of it. Doesn't belong to any golf clubs, hasn't got a lot of friends up around here from what I can gather. Very big on her gym membership, keeping trim.'

'She keeps trim all right,' said Clarissa. 'This is when you hate being this age, isn't it? You see them prance in front of you—what is she, twenty-three?—I mean, she nearly turned Alan's head; she's that good-looking.' Ross gave Clarissa a scowl.

'What does that say about her?' asked Macleod.

'All about herself,' said Hope, 'but she's not in the line for the first killing, and she was up at the golf club for the second one.'

'Unlike Cecil Ayers, though,' said Jona, 'she certainly would have the ability to have carried out the killings. Cecil Ayers is too old.'

'Who else have we got?

'Well,' said Ross, 'Alastair Begley's previously run a sports club. He's happily married with a family. I can't find any dirt, particularly, on him. He's just a normal, happily married man. He likes his golf. People here say he's a little bit intense at times, but he does a decent job. He has every reason to be here. He also doesn't want the tour to be here so it seems bizarre he would kill anybody.

'Padrick O'Reilly, well, we all know about him and his affair with Orla Smith. He worked in Ireland in various golf clubs before he got his opportunity here,' said Ross. 'Three years ago, he came. Apparently, he's done a good job. He's well-liked by the members, prior to the infidelity coming out. Although,

I spoke to a few people back in Ireland and they said that they weren't surprised at his adultery. It appears Mr O'Reilly is a man that likes his women.'

'It's a wonder he doesn't like Amy Johnson then,' said Clarissa. 'You'd think she would be turning his head, not Orla Smith.'

'You could give the man some credit,' said Macleod suddenly. 'We're not all chasing after the newest-looking thing in the block. Some men do appreciate women beyond their looks. Orla Smith was a quiet soul from what I've heard, efficient. People like that sometimes can be quite good listeners. That might have attracted him. I don't know what his wife's like.'

'All of which doesn't get us anywhere,' said Hope. 'What about our two deceased parties?'

'Well,' said Ross, 'Sandy Mackintosh had a stable marriage before his wife died five years ago. Always the golf man, always with clubs, and in the sport as a good amateur. He lived and breathed golf, especially after she'd died. Good friends with Andrew Peters. People say that the two of them used to come up here with their wives—the last twenty or twenty-five years. Always the mainstays at the club socials. A lot of the members said to me that it's not surprising that Peters was upset by Mackintosh's death.'

'What about Orla?' asked Hope.

'No golf connections before getting this job,' said Ross. 'Hired and voted in, basically to tighten up the ship with regards to the staff, which by all means, she has. Everything looks shipshape. I've gone through the books, I've gone through what's going on with the staff, and I don't hear many bad words about her.'

'Anything else?' asked Macleod.

155

'She was a keen gardener. Kept herself to herself up here, worked in the garden. This seems to be such a social hub for these people. This was their life. It's a big part of what they do.'

'That means it's something worth killing over,' said Hope. She looked over at Macleod but noticed he was rather distracted. He was off thinking again. He did that in meetings at times, even when he was running them. That's why he liked Hope to be there at the bigger ones.

'Well, we've got to dig deeper, folks, because we need to make something break. As it stands, the board is three and three now. They need another two to get to a dormie five and for a vote to happen.'

'They won't kill two more people,' said Macleod.

'They only need to kill one, Seoras,' said Clarissa. 'They've already bumped off the free place. Bump another one and away you go.'

'I'm not so sure,' said Macleod. 'I spoke to Dermot McKinley. I'm not sure how the tour is going to take this. There are always other golf courses. I know they say that all publicity is good, but I'm not sure it applies in this instance.'

'Okay,' said Hope. 'Boots on the ground. Clarissa, get back amongst the staff. See if we can tie anyone outside of the board to the killings. Where was everybody? What were they doing?'

'Gone over this, Hope,' said Clarissa. 'Most of them weren't anywhere with anyone. You know what our problem is, don't you? The first killing, Amy Johnson can't have done it. She's got the alibi. Second killing, Peters seems unlikely, and O'Reilly's also off the hook for that one.'

'Why's Peters unlikely?'

'He said he was elsewhere. He's got a loose alibi. Timing-

156

wise, he could have got back, but it's a long hike and a lot to do. Not convinced,' said Clarissa.

'Then we need to put pressure on. We need something to break. We've got a clock ticking. There may not be another murder,' said Hope, 'but somebody's got to be dislodged. I hope Seoras is right. I hope they understand that if they do kill too many people, they'll scare the tour off. If it's not that, then there may be another murder. We need to find out that link before it happens.'

Chapter 17

Macleod left the golf club in an odd mood. Something was bothering him about the case. The way in which the two murders had been a little bit different and yet looked similar. Was it a copycat? They were struggling to find one motive, never mind two. The motive of the tour and the attraction of its money was certainly strong, but how to enact that, balancing up the murders against the horror the tour would feel about the course after that. Of course, the tour wouldn't arrive for a year or two after, at least. While there was a rush to get the deal done, the stigma could disappear by that time, if it wasn't linked to the actual tour coming.

Part of him was itching to get back in there and detail what the troops should do, but Hope was doing a good job. It wasn't about her inadequacy. It was about his discombobulation. He was out of sync. DCI? He'd never been the DCI. He was never born to be sitting above everyone else. He was always the man out in front. It's what he was good at.

Paperwork, people—that wasn't him. Yes, he knew why it wasn't him. The death of his wife taking him to Glasgow, all those years of funnelling himself into the job, whilst quite frankly being a prig to women in general, but he'd changed from that. He'd like to think that these days he might still be a grumpy one, but at least he was a more tolerant person, more embracing, and certainly a lot more respectful to women.

It wasn't always easy to drag yourself into the modern age, and there was some of the modern age he didn't think he should be dragging himself into, but he had certainly moved on from where he was before. Grown, that's what they say, isn't it? At all these seminars or self-help groups, you've grown. You've been on the journey. He hated the rhetoric. He just sorted himself out with a little help. Not every man needed a good woman, but he did. He was just lucky to have found one.

As he reached the car, Macleod heard his phone ring, reached down, and answered it.

'Hello, Inspector. This is Dermot McKinley. I need to speak to you. I need to understand what's going on. There's a lot of pressure here at the moment. Two deaths, Inspector.'

'What's your main concern, sir? Because if it's to do with the club, that really is a private matter.'

'Probably best if we speak in private. I can meet you at the same hotel if you wish. Would you be available?'

'I can make myself available,' said Macleod. 'When do you wish to get together?'

'I'll buy you lunch, Inspector. Same hotel?'

Macleod wasn't keen on the hotel, but he wasn't going to go through a list of suggestions. After all, he was a policeman, and no doubt Mr. McKinley would be looking for a little bit of inside information.

'Same hotel will be fine,' said Macleod. 'Shall we say eleven-thirty?

'Rather early for lunch, Inspector.'

'I thought we could discuss first and then have lunch afterwards. A little bit more pleasant than discussing this matter when there's food involved.'

'I thought your stomach would be well attuned to that sort of thing.'

'Eleven-thirty it is,' said Macleod, and closed the call. He got annoyed when people assumed that he was immune to the distastefulness of the matters he investigated. Just because he saw it, didn't mean that he had built up a thick skin. He had learned how to cope with it in the immediate sense, but it always took a toll. A toll that very few ever said or acknowledged.

He certainly acknowledged it more these days, even if only to Jane. The team didn't know he'd had treatment, as it was put, for the most recent cases. Being trapped underwater with Clarissa had affected him more than he'd realised, not his own imminent death, as he subsequently found out with his counsellor, but the fact he'd nearly lost her. Still, that was behind him. This case seemed to convey a lot less risk to force than to the board members.

Macleod returned to the station, and after two hours of what seemed like endless paperwork and his secretary badgering him to sign off more sheets, Macleod drove down to the hotel on the outskirts of Inverness. He arrived punctually, eleven-thirty, and found Dermot McKinley already there. The man was nursing a whisky.

'I take it you won't want one if you're on duty, or can I?'

'Mr McKinley,' said Macleod, putting his hand forward and then shaking Dermot's, 'I don't drink. Lewis born and bred, had it knocked out of me. I hear that it's not the case with a lot of us.'

'Knowing a few from up that way, I'd say your assessment is fair,' said McKinley. 'You don't mind if . . .'

'No. As long as you keep your head, there's no problem from me.' Macleod wondered what his previous occupants of the job had done. Did some of them come and get drunk? Surely not. He was going to say they were police officers after all, but considering the last occupant, he really didn't want to give any ground to their supposed propriety.

Dermot McKinley waited until Macleod's coffee had arrived, breaking the silence with some banal chatter about his life on the tour. Macleod wasn't really listening, but when the man leaned forward, Macleod understood that the juicy detail was coming.

'I'm under pressure. A lot of pressure.'

'That's sad to hear,' said Macleod, 'but I'm really not seeing how that's my issue.'

'It's the bosses, you see. The bosses are looking to make a deal on this tour event. They want it done before everything gets out of hand.'

'That's an awful big assumption, isn't it?' said Macleod. 'Quite frankly, a rather dark one.'

'You mean the assumption that these killings are to do with our arrival? Well, yes. Frankly, it is. I'm not happy about it. I'm just the messenger on this one, Macleod; don't shoot me.'

'Do you have any evidence that it is?'

'That's why I was wanting to talk to you. Do you have evidence?'

Macleod leaned back in his chair, his hand nursing his coffee. 'If I had evidence,' said Macleod, 'I would be acting on that evidence. The last thing I would do is come to yourself with it. Understand this, Mr McKinley, I like you. You're a decent

161

man. We can talk quite happily; I can give general overviews. But if you're specifically asking me if these murders are to do with the vote on the tour, I will make no comment.'

'It's more than that,' said McKinley. 'You see, really they're wanting to know, can they get it passed beforehand? It could be good for you, too. If the matter was sorted, the killings would stop. That would be good, wouldn't it?'

Macleod nearly jumped in and said 'It's nothing to do with yourself, and whether the killings stop or not is not the point.' Maybe it was the point. Maybe he needed to get the killings to stop. After all, that's what he was as a policeman. He was always concerned about the next person, not just the bodies that had fallen.

'What have you done about it?' asked Macleod. 'What have you done about it that it's coming to me? You know I'm a police officer. You know I probably won't speak, and yet you're talking to me. What have you done?'

'It's not that easy going in to talk. The Board wouldn't want me in there. That would be seen as influencing the decision. I can't talk to the members because that would be influencing the decision as well. It's an exciting course. It's perfect. A good part of the world. We can get good grants if we get the competition going, and then who knows beyond that? Who knows what that course could be used for? This is Inverness. It's on the up. You're aware of that, aren't you, Inspector?'

Macleod had indeed seen Inverness grow around him, but he wasn't quite sure why that should affect his judgment.

'There's an awful lot to consider here. The fact the tour is still involved shows how important this course is to us, Inspector. I hope that you appreciate that.'

'I can certainly understand it. Appreciate is probably too

strong a word,' said Macleod.

'I've spoken to Amy Johnson,' said Dermot. 'She said that the Club Secretary vote had gone through. She said there was three on each side now, another position to come up. I asked her how she was going to get the main vote passed, but from what I could gather, the mood in the club, or certainly on the Board, wasn't good even if the members were for it.

'I think the board's out of touch. Alastair Begley, who I have a lot of respect for, is wrong on this one. The club could do with this. It's their new model. You don't have clubs the old way now. They need to look forward to how to make money. People don't want to go round the same course. The people with money want to travel around. They want to be looked after. Corporate, that's where the money is.'

'I feel there's a few at the golf club who disagree with you on that one,' said Macleod, 'but you talked about the fact that it was three and three. How was Miss Johnson going to get a dormie five?'

'She said she was going to push through another vote. They have to have seven board members.'

'Indeed,' said Macleod, 'but even if she got somebody who was pro-the-tour coming in, you still have a problem. That would be four against three. You need five. You need five for a vote, and the tour is getting jittery.'

'Yes, Inspector, they are. I believe she was looking to change someone's mind.'

Macleod sat back again, looked out the window, and he could feel the unease of Dermot McKinley.

'You're worried, sir, aren't you? You're worried about what you've got yourselves into. Why not just cut ties? Why not just run? Plenty of other golf courses, aren't there?'

163

'No, there's not, Inspector. Not this one. There's a lot of grants that go into this. Amy's quite something. She's worked a lot of money coming our way to help fund the tour event, but also promote it in the promise that we will come back and lift the status of the event. Unlike our own Open, other tournaments don't have to be on a links course. Other events, more prestigious events, don't. Some of my bosses have very vested interests in these other events. I'm bringing them there. They're seeing Amy as someone they can work with.'

'Will her stature be lifted by this? asked Macleod. 'I mean, at the moment she's . . .'

'She's just a club publicity officer,' said Dermot. 'Frankly, I'm worried, Macleod. That's why you're talking to me. I'd rather that what I'm about to say didn't go anywhere.'

'Go on,' said Macleod. 'If it's something incriminating, I can't guarantee that.'

'I don't think it is. What I do know is that if she pulls this off, she may be looking at a position in the tour. Well, not in the tour. More around the tour and to be one of the companies making the events happen.'

'A lot of money,' said Macleod.

'Oh, the money's there, but that's not the thing. It's more to do with the prestige. She's all about prestige.'

'Do you feel she's someone who would break limits to get the job done, so to speak?'

'I have no idea if she'd murdered someone,' said Dermot, suddenly pulling back. Macleod saw for a moment a tinge of fear.

'You're not sure, are you?' said Macleod. 'Why is that? What's making you think that?' A blush came across the man's face. 'How connected are you to her?' asked Macleod.

'Professionally, I'm just—'

'Not professionally,' interrupted Macleod. 'How attached to her are you? What's come between you? What has . . .'

The man's face went redder, and his eyes dipped down. 'It shouldn't have happened,' said Dermot suddenly.

'What do you mean it shouldn't have happened?'

'I knew that our people were happy about the course. I'd played it and gave it a glowing report. You never give your cards away in this game, Inspector. You always keep them back just in case things don't go right. She was worried, I think. She was worried after we'd had a meeting. I'd brought some of our people in to meet her and to meet the Board. The issue of the vote had come up, and to be honest, it looked like it was going to kill the deal. I was speaking to her afterwards because I'd put a lot of work into it. So had she. I thought the course was ideal, but I didn't let that be known.'

'She did what?' asked Macleod.

'She propositioned me right there and then.'

'You accepted?'

'I accepted then, and I accepted several more times.'

'Has she used that connection?' asked Macleod.

'She did last time. Told me I had to keep the board involved. It's a form of blackmail. It's done, Macleod. Doesn't prove murder though. I just felt someone should know and I couldn't tell my bosses, and you, well, you seem like someone who might understand.'

Macleod wasn't quite sure how to take this. He'd never done something like that in his life. He'd like to feel he had a bit more integrity.

'What's going to be the game-changer though? You've kept the talks going. They haven't said that they're out yet. Your bosses are still in. You've let it be known to me that this course is important to you. Does Amy know that?'

'Not to that extent.'

'She thinks that you are on the verge of pulling out.'

'Exactly. I've told her about the situation, and I've said that our Board will cut and run if the club's management issues come up. If these killings are all about what happens inside the running of the club, we can't touch it. Even after two or three years, we couldn't touch it. If it just happens to be a killer that kills on a golf course, leaves this macabre image, well, that isn't bad publicity that's going to be our problem.'

Macleod wondered what to do. He needed to think.

'Mr. McKinley, I will keep this conversation within my colleagues' circle, but I can't keep it private forever. If I need to bring it out, I will. In the meantime, I would suggest you refrain from having relations with that lady. As for lunch, I'll get my own. With what you've told me, I can't have you buying me things.'

Macleod stood up, thanked the man, and walked out to his car. He drove until he found a good coffee shop where he picked up a sandwich and sat down on the banks of the River Ness. He couldn't sit in the office, not his new office, and look out that window over the town, because it faced the wrong way. He'd sit here. After all, if he went to his old office, he'd disturb Hope's team, even though she wasn't there.

He had a problem. Amy Johnson had an alibi for the first killing. What was going on? He'd finish his sandwich and report his findings to Hope.

Chapter 18

Hope looked up from rereading Jona's report as Clarissa marched into the small office they held in the clubhouse. The woman seemed to be slightly flustered, as if she'd raced over to Hope, her cheeks rosy red, huffing and puffing beneath her shawl.

'You're not going to believe this.'

'Not believe what?' asked Hope.

'They're holding a board meeting. They're actually holding a board meeting. According to Frank, they're trying to push forward. How does this work? Have we got somebody on the wrong side here? Is somebody not showing their true colours because frankly, how are you going to sit down as a board and vote through to get things done?'

'They're down in the boardroom at the moment?' asked Hope. Clarissa nodded. 'Right,' she said and stood up, marching out of the room.

'Where are you off?' called Clarissa.

'I want to be in that board meeting!'

'Yes, but how are you going to do that?'

'I'm going to knock on the door and walk in and you're coming with me.'

'I'm coming with you?'

'Well, they kept calling you Macleod's Rottweiler. Don't see why you can't do the same for me.'

Hope didn't look back, no idea how that comment would be taken, but she could hear the heavy breath of Clarissa following her down the stairs and round to the boardroom. Hope on arrival thundered a fist on the door and barged in.

'Detective Sergeant, you can't just march into a board meeting,' said Andrew Peters. 'We are in session.'

'Fine. As soon as you're out of session, I will haul each of you in here and get you to explain to me what has been said at this meeting. We have significant evidence to say that these deaths are linked to the decisions made in this boardroom, so you can all either sit with me for the rest of the day and go through what you've discussed once you come out, or I can sit in. I won't interfere. I won't say anything, but it'll save me having to say anything else or hold you for the rest of the day. I mean, I take it it's all minuted.'

'Of course, it's minuted,' said Peters. He pointed to a woman at the back of the room. A shy lady with glasses, possibly in her late sixties, sat with a pad of paper.

'Good, but I want it first hand, because that's what I'd be asking you about. If you don't mind, I'll take two more chairs please.'

Peters looked around.

'Well, why not,' said O'Reilly. 'What have you got to fear from them? I haven't got anything to fear from them. They know I didn't do anything.'

'Are you insinuating that somebody here did?' Peters was up now on his feet, fists down on the table, staring at O'Reilly.

'Bloody well seems like it, doesn't it?'

'Let them stay,' said Cecil. 'I'm not for sitting around for the rest of the day. Let them stay, but please, Sergeant, don't talk to the other members, please, if you respect our privacy. I understand if it comes up in the investigation, you must use it, but outside of that, can we rely on your discretion?'

'Of course,' said Hope. 'If it doesn't pertain to the investigation, it won't be used.'

Peters shot a look over to Cecil and shook his head like this was a bad idea but then he acquiesced.

'All right. All right. Somebody go and get some seats, but at the back, please, and I'll hold you to your word not to say anything. This is our discussion. This is us. I don't want questions in the middle. You have questions, hold them until after. We need to get this business done.'

Hope turned with an angry face, and then walked over to Peters. The man sat down as she approached, which she enjoyed as she stared down at him from her height.

'This is a murder investigation. You mess me about, and I will do everything in my power to stop these meetings happening. I'll call a halt to everything. I will use every injunction I can, every reason. I will pull my forensic team in here for a sweep. I will make everything so difficult for you to operate if you mess me about. Am I clear?'

The hands on the hips was probably an overindulgence, but Hope was sure that the man knew where the rules lay.

'Of course, of course,' said Peters suddenly. 'Where are those seats?'

The lady who had been doing the minutes disappeared out of the room into a small side room and brought in two comfortable seats. She had difficulty carrying them and Clarissa raced over to help her before she and Hope sat at

169

the rear of the room. The large table had seven seats, one unoccupied. Clearly it wasn't going to be given to Hope or Clarissa.

'Now the motion before us is to allow for a temporary board member in the position of staff manager so that we can get a vote completed in the next couple of days rather than leave it for weeks.'

Hope put her hand up.

'What is it?' said Peters.

'Can you just explain to me what the hell you mean?' said Hope.

'He's bypassing it,' said Pádraig O'Reilly. 'We have the rule that we have to get the positions filled quickly. That's correct, but Orla Smith held a paid position. Therefore, yes, you get to vote in someone on it, but you have to also go through all the normal employment procedures. We're bypassing that and saying we're going to get a club member to come in and run that position, temporarily. Thereby, a vote can happen. Otherwise, the person strictly isn't in place for another three weeks or so. He's worried that the tour by that point will have told him to shove it up his arse.'

'I don't think you can talk to anyone, O'Reilly, after where you were shoving it,' yelled Peters.

'Really,' said Cecil. 'That's not how we behave. This is a board meeting. Ladies, I do apologise.'

Hope glanced at Clarissa, and then looked over at Amy and then the woman who was taking notes. She thought the only person Cecil could really be apologising to was the woman taking notes. Clarissa and Hope had heard much worse, and she was pretty sure that Amy wasn't behind the door with comments. In fact, Hope reckoned that Clarissa had probably said worse.

'Can we get down to business?' asked Cecil.

'It's not normal procedure, but we need to vote on this. This can't be decided by a lack of a board being in place. Things are being driven,' said Peters. 'Being driven by the outside, and we can't just let this club lurch along because we didn't act.'

'He is right,' said Cecil. 'I'd rather have a vote on this than having no vote, and then forever it gets said that the board didn't act, the board didn't take charge. This should be our decision, however that decision goes.'

'Bollocks,' said O'Reilly. 'Absolute bollocks. That's what they're wanting. They're wanting to force someone else in. They get the right person in and it's four to three. You wait and see. One of us is up next.'

'How dare you imply somebody here is killing off people? Orla was a beloved member. Orla was loved by all,' said Peters.

Hope noticed that Amy didn't say much, but she took in every detail. Peters, on the other hand, was in his element. Maybe this is where he worked. Maybe being in the board-room was what suited him.

'Can I just remind everyone,' said Amy, 'that the tour has stated that if the publicity comes out about the murders, they may be forced to pull out, so we really do need to make a quick decision. This vote is not unreasonable, is it, Alastair?'

The gaunt Alastair Begley looked up and Hope thought he was going to be physically sick. The man had never looked in the best of health since she'd arrived, but right at this moment, he looked positively white.

'No,' he said. 'I agree with Cecil. This needs to be decided by us. Given that there's only the six of us, we can make a decision.'

'Or we can block that bloody stupid decision,' said O'Reilly.

'Pádraig,' said Cecil Ayres, 'I know you're upset. We all loved Orla.'

'Some people loved her more than others,' said Peters.

'That's not helpful,' said Cecil. The older man seemed deeply aggrieved that such a discussion was going on. Hope thought she could see a tear in his eye.

'Pádraig, as much as I hate to say this, we do need to make a decision. It's right at this time to vote, and even though there's not seven of us, there's only six, there is express permission to do something like this. It's not a major decision.'

'It will cause a major decision, though. It causes a major decision. It's not right.'

'It is allowable though,' said Cecil. 'And I believe it's right.'

'Can we vote, then? Can we damn well vote?' implored Andrew Peters. 'All in favour of allowing the post of Staff Manager to be put up and for a club member to take that post without pay and act, as such, as a board member in the interim until we advertise fully for that position, say aye.'

Hope watched five arms go up as aye was murmured. Andrew Peters, Cecil Ayres, Amy Johnson, Alastair Begley, and the newly elected Jim Durbin.

'Everyone who says nay.'

Pádraig put his hand up with a resounding 'Nay!'

'Motion is passed. Let the minutes reflect so. That being so, we shall put invitations out this afternoon for those who wish to stand, and I say that we still have an election as soon as possible.'

'I'm going to fight this,' said Pádraig. 'If we're going to have candidates, we'll damn well have candidates, ones that will tell you where to put it.'

'And I'll be with you,' said Alastair Begley. 'And me,' said Cecil. 'This deal won't happen. You can flash your eyes all you want, Miss Johnson. You're not what this club needs. Those golfers that want to come and see something sexy, they can clear off. This club is about tradition. This club is about our place in the history books. This club is about that links course, not this new-fangled American nonsense.'

Hope watched as Andrew Peters broke up the meeting, but as he did so, she saw Amy Johnson reaching into her pocket and pulling out her phone. A wry smile came on the woman's lips. She stood up and walked round to Pádraig O'Reilly, holding up the phone in front of his face. Hope saw him stare for a minute. His face went white.

'You bastards. Who the hell leaked this? You bastards. Did you leak it?' He turned to Hope who stood up.

'No,' she said. 'I'm not in the business of doing that. Whatever dirty work's gone on here, it's got nothing to do with me or my officers.'

He turned back to Johnson and looked over at Peters. 'It's you, you bastards. It's you, you bastards, but you won't chase me off here. I won't resign on things like that.'

As he walked past, Amy Johnson said over her shoulder to him, 'You may not get the choice. Members aren't going to like it.'

Hope thought she saw a deep smile forming on the face of Amy Johnson, but the woman turned away before she could approach her. Alastair Begley rushed out after O'Reilly while Cecil Ayers sat back in his chair, breathing heavily, his eyes now looking sodden.

'Is this what you wanted, Peters? Is this really what you wanted?' said the old man.

'It's not my fault if you can't see the future. You can't have this old-style club. It won't work. It won't work anymore. Bloody idiots.'

Peters grabbed his folder from the front of the table, turned on his heel, and gave a scowl to Hope. 'Well, I hope that's given you enough,' and he marched out of the room.

Clarissa leaned over to Hope as the rest of the board filed out. 'Spicy, aren't they? That makes our sort of little get-togethers seem dull.'

'Find me where that leak came from,' said Hope. 'There's dirty fighting going on here. Talk to your man, Frank. Find me what the hell's going on. Get me the inside scoop on who's going to be voted up. See if anybody's trashing O'Reilly. Things are afoot here. It may not end up in another death, but it could show us who committed the last ones.'

She watched Clarissa stand, a determination on her face. She thought this was what it must have been like for Macleod when you took off the chain and let the Rottweiler go. 'Use their strength,' he had said. 'Rely on your team,' but she needed to know more. She needed to understand where Peters was coming from. Could he be a killer? He was an overweight sixty-year-old and retired. Maybe he wasn't in the best of shape, but neither was Sandy Mackintosh and as for madam, she thought, Amy Johnson was an operator. Just what sort? She had an alibi. Was she simply the fuel on the fire or was she actively stoking it up?

Chapter 19

'Seoras, where are you?'

'I'm all for informality, Hope, but you can ask me a little bit better than that. I am the acting DCI.'

'Enough. I'm not being funny. Where are you?'

'Out of the office. Doing a bit of thinking. What do you need?'

'They've only gone and had a board meeting. They've now opened the way for more elections to take place because Orla Smith's position as the staff manager was a paid position. What's meant to happen is you are interviewed and you're provisionally offered the job and the board votes them in, followed by the membership. They've changed that. They've had a meeting and they've changed it. Even the daft sods who don't want anything to happen have changed it, because they want seven. They want a decision. Everybody wants a decision made on this tour coming. All I see is more opportunity and more reason for somebody to take things into their own hands.'

'I understand that,' said Macleod. 'Why are you calling me, precisely?

'We've got to get everything cancelled. I was in the board meeting today. Peters drives everything. Andrew Peters is the force behind their meetings and in making sure the club runs. He may want this tour in, but he is also very much about the club, and he pushes things forward. It's a bizarre thing. You want different things, but yet at times they seem to be coming together. Only Padraig O'Reilly voted against the proposal they had today.'

'Well, he's seen somebody die that's close to him.'

'The others have too,' said Hope. 'Sandy Mackintosh was a good friend of them all. Why can't they see that this is potentially going to lead to another murder?'

'It's the way they are. Once again, what is it you want from me?'

'I need you to go and talk to Andrew Peters.'

'Why?' asked Macleod. 'Can't you do that? I handed the case over to you, Hope. This is yours to run with. Stamp your authority on it.'

'It's not about that, Seoras. It's about the way Andrew Peters works. He'd pull the seats out for the women. I think Amy Johnson must play him like crazy. He's very old-school. Man's man in some ways.'

'You're not allowed to say that these days,' said Macleod. 'That's offensive.'

'Stop messing about, Seoras. I'm serious. I need you to go and talk to him. He might actually listen to you. Also, you're the DCI. He'd like a visit from the big wigs. Might listen to you more than the little old sergeant.'

'You're using me as part of the team?'

'Yes. I don't want you to take over. I just want you to do this for me. How did you ever stay so calm?' said Hope suddenly. 'How did you ever manage it? You get all these things going this way and that while you're trying to make something happen.'

'You're ultimately carrying the can for it. Yes, I know,' said Macleod. 'I stayed calm, because if I didn't, I'd probably hit somebody. It's what we need to do. You don't get there by getting all worked up. Even when they rile you bad. You get there by using your brain. You get there by thinking through what needs to happen and then doing it. I'll go and talk to Andrew Peters. It's the right move. If he's as you describe, we've got a chance, but I'm not saying it's going to work.'

'Thanks, Seoras.'

'Is John back yet?'

'Yes. Came back the other day. Saw him last night.'

'Good. You need somebody to talk it out with. You need somebody to listen. You don't have to tell them about the case, but you need somebody there. I've got Jane. You've got John. Make sure you use him. Make sure you involve him. He'll be able to tell you when you're going off the rails, when you've stretched too far. He'll bring you back. You can't do that with me. I'm too involved in the cases.'

'When are you going to see him?' asked Hope.

'I'm on my way, all right? Just let me finish off here and I'll be there. I'll give you a call when I'm done.'

'Thanks, Seoras. I owe you one.'

'No, you don't. Part of the team. Helping you out. Less of that, please.'

Macleod was delighted about having to see Andrew Peters. He was looking at a drab office afternoon and another pestering from his secretary to get more paperwork done. How could there be so much paperwork? He'd felt it the first year he was a DI, but not like this? Most of it didn't refer to the present cases and he had to check through statistics and not just the important ones like crimes solved or detected, but more and more details about policing policies and communications to other departments, where his budget was spent, how that tied in with forensics. Oh, it was just mind numbing.

He was also enjoying driving the car. He usually got taken everywhere, but today he was out in his own. The sky was a clear blue, cold but clear. There were still bits of snow lying around, but surely spring was on the way soon. Macleod looked up Andrew Peters's house upon arrival and found it to be dark and empty.

He knocked on the door several times before making a circuitous route around the property three times, for it was substantial. *Too much for one man*, he thought. As he was making his last circuit, a head popped up from over the neighbouring fence.

'Who the hell are you?' asked a voice. Macleod stopped walking. 'Oh, it's you, isn't it? What are you doing here? Is it to do with the golf club?'

Macleod gave a sigh and walked over to the man. He had curly brown hair, was middle-aged, and looked slightly unkempt. Macleod was trying to patch how this man was living in a house, which seemed to be a similar size to Andrew Peters, when he saw somebody else approaching from behind.

'Come on, stop it. Don't bother the man.'

'But it's Macleod. It's Macleod. Look, I'm telling you. It's Macleod.'

'You think everybody's Macleod.'

Macleod looked over the fence and saw a woman running over. She seemed to be wearing scrubs, but Macleod suddenly put two and two together, realizing the man needed some help in life. He still didn't get why he had such a big house next door to Andrew Peters.

'Hello, there,' said Macleod. 'I am acting Detective Chief Inspector Macleod. How are you?

'God, it is. Isn't it?' said the woman. Macleod ignored the casual blasphemy.

'Yes, it is. I'm looking for Andrew Peters. He doesn't seem to be in. Do you know where he would be?'

'No, he's not, and I have no idea where he'd be,' said the woman.

'Cemetery. He'll be in the cemetery.'

'Stop it, Aron,' said the woman.

'He'll be in the cemetery. He always goes cemetery today. Off to see his wife.'

'Aron, Mr Macleod doesn't want to hear you babbling on . . '

'It's Inspector Macleod, and actually Aron's making a lot of sense. I don't know if you know, but Andrew Peters has lost his wife quite recently. It's quite likely he's up at the graveyard. Do you know which one it is, Aron?

'Local to here. Doesn't take long. Ten minutes maybe."

'Well, thank you, Aron,' said Macleod. He put his hand over the fence and Aron shook it, but at the same time began to jump up and down. 'It's Macleod. It's Macleod.'

'Aron,' said his agitated helper.

'It's perfectly fine,' said Macleod. 'You can call me Seoras. Thank you, Aron.'

'Thank you, Seoras,' said the man. There was something quite endearing about the man and Macleod smiled as he made his way back to the car. It was only a short drive up to the local cemetery. Macleod parked on the edge at the car park and walked in along the path, staring around at the gravestones. It brought back the memory of his wife's suicide in Lewis, and of the solitary gravestone over there.

Hope Macleod. He'd come a long way since then, but he always attributed his joy in life to the two women who had made it for him. Hope Macleod and now his Jane.

Macleod heard crying. It wasn't unusual to hear crying in a graveyard, but this wasn't that far away. He noticed that Andrew Peters was knelt down before a grave. Tears were running from the man's eyes as he adjusted flowers into a small pot sitting in front of a rather grandiose headstone. Macleod casually walked around to the back of the man and stood patiently waiting.

When the man started to speak to his wife, Macleod walked off. He stayed about forty yards away, unable to hear the quiet talk believing that he should at least give the man that respect. Maybe he was confessing to something. Maybe he was talking about the situation. Maybe he was just lonely and needed to chat. It didn't matter. He was talking to his deceased wife. He deserved the respect. When Andrew Peters stood up, Macleod made his move and just as the man turned around, he caught Macleod standing less than five feet away.

'Mr. Peters, I hope you'll forgive the intrusion. I did see you were talking to your wife. I stood well away. I didn't hear anything.'

'Thank you, Inspector. People nowadays are not decent, are they?

'No, I find that sometimes. I need to talk to you about what's going on.'

'What's going on is what needs to happen, Inspector. That's the thing, isn't it? They'll see it as a betrayal. They haven't seen the real betrayal.'

'What is the real betrayal?'

Andrew Peters bowed by his head. 'We need to protect this club. The good things in life need protecting. We need to look after it. Times are changing. Things are not the way they used to be.

'I used to come up to that club with Sandy Mackintosh. We would've taken both our wives with us. That's the days when a husband could take his wife out to the club. Oh, we had laughs. There was dancing sometimes, bingo nights, there was all sorts of things. Nowadays it's all changed, hasn't it? Changed from when we were young.

'Everybody was friends back then, but nowadays it's not the same. Need to get the money in, Inspector,' said the man suddenly. 'She's shown me that, Amy. I know what you're thinking. You're thinking that she's there because she looks good. Between you and me, Inspector, of course she does. If she offered, you wouldn't say no, would you?'

'Frankly, I would,' said Macleod, 'but I have my own partner.'

'Yes. Well, I'm afraid you're one of a dying breed. You don't get much respect these days. You can't hang on to tradition either, can you? Besides, what is tradition? It's just one person's side of it. One person's view or interpretation. They all tell you they're holding on to real things in this life. The things that matter. They're not. They're just taking what they want. Most of them didn't give the course a chance. It's a stunning course. It's what people want. The corporates will come, they'll give us plenty of money. The members still have the links and they can play the other course. We get the tour there and the money will come in.'

'I thought tour events could be a mixed bag,' said Macleod.

'They can be, but this won't be. Not with Amy on board. She's good. She's very good. Going to give the young a chance.

181

That's the thing, us old ones, we think about the old style and we think it's all right and proper and couldn't go wrong. The old things go wrong, Macleod. They really do.'

'We're not just talking about things going wrong, though, are we, sir?' said Macleod. 'People have died. Somebody seems to be influencing this. Somebody seems to be pushing an agenda.'

'You think that someone is me?'

'I don't know what to think about you,' said Macleod. 'You're definitely that old school style. My sergeant told me about the meeting. You really stand up, shout them down. Somebody leaked about Padraig O'Reilly. Now that's a nasty move.'

'It's not nasty. What he did to his wife was nasty. You ever been betrayed?'

Macleod shook his head. 'Only widowed,' he said.

'It's bad enough, isn't it? What about Padraig's wife? She's the one stuck on the outside. She's the one that doesn't get a say in it. No. He ran around and then he's crying over his dame because she's got murdered. I used to think something of her. Do you know that, Macleod? I used to think well of Orla Smith, but now I see what she's been up to.'

'She'll not be up to much more,' said Macleod. 'She's dead.'

'Maybe the wife did that one.'

'But then who did for Mackintosh?' asked Macleod. 'We need to halt this. I know the tour won't want another death. At worst, by what you've done, you've invited the killer out again. You do get that, don't you?'

'We're not doing this to entice a killer. We're doing this because it's what needs to be done. Sometimes things need to be taken in hand, Inspector. Sometimes things get too much. Sometimes you need to go on. Now, if you don't mind, I'd like a few more words with my wife.'

Macleod nodded and walked away. As he marched across the grass towards his car, he swore he heard the man spit. When he turned back, Andrew Peters was an upright figure, head bowed. Macleod turned back.

When he got to the car, he felt unusually chilled. *Something, something was there*, he thought. *In that conversation, something was there. What was it?* He could feel everything within him pointing to something. He just didn't know what.

Chapter 20

Hope desperately wanted to go out to interview. Being the hub, the centre of information flow, was difficult. She was solving a case in a different way to how she was used to. This case, as well, was awkward. There was nowhere to rush to. They weren't hunting down a killer on the move. Instead, they were having to sift through people who didn't look like killers. They looked like ordinary people, angry, agitated, wanting their own way, yes, but not killers. If only it had been clearer, if the chase had been on. But there was no chase. Hope was a woman of action; she wasn't Macleod. She'd need to be there, need to be ready for it. She felt the mobile vibrating, picked it up, put it to her ear.

'Hope, Clarissa here. Pádraig is missing.'

'What do you mean?'

'Pádraig is missing. The groundsman said to me he was meant to be coming over to talk to him this afternoon. They go through different things about the holes and make sure everything's growing properly. Anyway, what came out of it was he never turned up, so Frank phoned him, no answer. He's phoned the house and Pádraig's wife doesn't know where he is.'

The hairs rose on Hope's neck.

'Go and get help. Get a search going.'

'Is it not a bit early for that?' asked Clarissa.

'No. They put all the story out about his affair. He's in a vulnerable situation and nobody knows where he is. We need to track him down. I'm not happy with this one. This is not a wait-and-see, Clarissa; get on it now. Talk to Ross, get people moving. If you have trouble getting the numbers for searching, then come back to me. Your priority is to find Pádraig now.'

'Understood,' said Clarissa. 'I'll let you know as soon as I have something.'

Hope closed the call and popped the phone back in her jeans pocket. Pádraig was livid and shocked when the information got out about his infidelity. Hope wondered what he had been like before. She looked over at Ross in the corner. Any minute now, he'd probably get a phone call from Clarissa, so she called him over.

'Ross, Clarissa is going to call you. Pádraig is missing. I need you to help her sort out manpower, but let her run it. Give her whatever assistance she needs.'

'Will do.'

'The other thing is, Ross, when you spoke to the Irish contacts about Pádraig O'Reilly, you said they weren't surprised. Get back onto them. Find out for me if he was ever caught or if his wife ever knew.'

'On it,' said Ross, before she'd turned away. She heard him bashing the buttons of the phone. Hope stepped outside trying to collect her thoughts as to what to do next. From there, she walked down the stairs around to the small office of Amy Johnson. The woman was sitting in a rather smart, and slightly revealing, blouse, tussling her hair as she studied her computer.

Hope knocked on the door, saw the woman look over, and almost gave a frown before waving her in.

'What can I do for you, Sergeant?'

How she made the word sergeant sound derogatory, Hope didn't know. She wasn't going to rise to the bait; there were more important things at stake.

'We need to call a halt to this,' said Hope. 'There's too much at stake; people have died.'

'But business is business. If we don't go through with this, if we don't go ahead, this club will die. What's that going to do for the memory of Sandy Mackintosh, Orla Smith?'

'We can cut the bull,' said Hope. 'I've seen you before; you're an operator. You're all about the money on this. Don't try and pretend it's for any of the golfing side of things. Orla Smith had more golf interest than you do. It's only the money that's pulled you here.'

'Well, since cards are on the table, why should we pull away? You're no closer to anything. You don't know who the murderer is or what they are doing? You don't know if there's going to be another murder. You don't know if any of these people have something in their past. You don't know if Riley's wife didn't turn round and kill Orla Smith. Sandy Mackintosh, didn't he have gambling debts? You have no idea what's going on, have you?'

Hope fixed a stare at the woman. 'Inquiries are proceeding,' she said calmly. 'What I need to do is to make sure that no further deaths occur, and the abandonment of this vote is the sure-fire way to stop that.'

'You don't know that, and you're going to make this club miss out on multi-millions. This club will be something and we're all agreed. You're the only ones wanting to stop at the moment.'

'You weren't all agreed, O'Reilly wasn't agreed.'

'O'Reilly's put himself in the mix. He's going to be in the papers, and he won't be on the board for much longer. It's not the image the club needs, is it?' Amy Johnson frowned.

'Somebody leaked that. There's an agenda going on here. There's an agenda that says we're going to take away our naysayers and we're going to put yes people in. Somebody's looking to kick out O'Reilly as well. What I don't get is why Orla Smith. Why not one of the others?'

'You know where I was anyway, so I don't understand why you're giving me such flak. It's not within my power to stop this going ahead. I'm a paid member of the board. I'm not one of the family, so to speak. You need to change all their minds, not just mine. I'm guessing you couldn't change Andrew Peters.'

'Why do you say that?' asked Hope.

'Because he knows what this means. He's dead set on it. He's about the only one with common sense on that board. The rest of them are all romantic idiots. Golf's changed; golf's moved on, like most of life. Dog-eat-dog world out there. You've got to be ready for it. Got to be prepared to do what it takes.'

Hope stared at the woman. It was funny that sometimes women dressed in a certain way and then people took the idea that the woman was easy as the parlance would go. *Women*, Hope thought, *could look at other women and know who was easy and who wasn't, however they were dressed*. Amy Johnson was not easy but Hope firmly believed that she could sleep with someone to further her own ends, even somebody she didn't particularly like. 'You need to stop, or you'll lose the chance. The tour will pull out at more killings.'

'That's the exact reason why we need to do it now,' said Amy Johnson. 'Delay is only going to cost us. At least the others had the decency to say it should be a vote, not just getting the rug pulled out from underneath us. Besides, it's already afoot; candidates are already being called. Two days' time, we're voting on a replacement. Four candidates have been put forward. You might say,' said Amy with a smile, 'there's two from either side. Plenty of choice for the members, but personally, I think one of our people will get in, somebody that'll say yes. That'll be four of us.'

'Still won't work though then,' said Hope, 'four, and a three. Unless somebody else is removed.'

'Things can happen,' said Amy, 'things can happen. That's one thing you learn. It's very hard to control things. It's very hard when everything's against you. You've got to stay tough.'

Hope didn't have a clue what the woman was talking about, but she wasn't getting anywhere either with her plan of making her see reason. Hope stormed back upstairs.

'Boss,' said Ross from the far side of the room, 'talked to people back in Ireland. Pádraig was never found out. Most of the guys knew what he was doing, what he was about, because he used to brag about it to them at a low level, but he never got caught.'

'That's interesting, Ross. That really is,' said Hope. But she also had a very strange feeling in her stomach as if what Ross had said painted a far darker picture.

She went over to the coffee machine, poured herself some coffee and stopped, as her mobile vibrated again.

'This is McGrath.'

'Hope, it's Seoras. I've spoken to Andrew Peters, haven't got a chance of changing his mind.'

'I got nowhere either, Seoras.'

'Are you going to have a try at Jim Durbin?'

'Could do, barely know the man. By the looks of it, he's a stooge put in anyway. I'll have to see what comes of the vote. I've just been told there's four candidates already put forward. They really are intent on doing this.'

'That's going to ratchet things up,' said Macleod. 'I'm going to head back to the office. Anything else I should know?'

'Pádraig O'Reilly's missing,' said Hope. 'I've got Clarissa organising a manhunt for him, but I've got a bad feeling.'

'How did he react when they outed him at the board meeting, when he found out he had the press down his neck?'

'Frightened. I got Ross to phone over to Ireland and they said back there he never got caught even though he was messing about.'

'That's not good,' said Macleod, 'that's really not good. I'm going to come to the club.'

'Why?'

'Bad feeling, Hope. Bad feeling and you'll need backup. You're going to need somebody to deflect what's going on. Stand at the front and take the flak from press, from golf club members, whoever. Can you feel it ramping up?'

'Yes,' she said, 'see you soon,' and closed down the call.

Hope walked over to the window of the room and looked down at the first tee beyond. There was nobody there, of course, with the course closed. *How did it get to this?* she thought. *How does it get to a little game with sticks and a ball and then up in a row, a deadly row? How on earth do you get killed over a game of golf?*

* * *

189

Clarissa was sitting on one of the groundstaff buggies beside Frank Macleod, the head groundsman. He was driving her along the course. She'd initially decided that the police would take outside of the course, checking around his house, any woods nearby, tracing down where the cars had gone. Ross had jumped onto CCTV and was coordinating that side of the work. But while they were gathering coastguards, mountain rescue, and anybody else they could come in and bring numbers for a search, Clarissa had asked the ground staff to do a quick run round the golf course.

Nobody had said Pádraig had gone home after the meeting. Nobody had said that he'd been in the bar either or around the club. His car was still in the club car park. Clarissa had a bad feeling and now, as she drove around the new course with Frank beside her, she didn't feel a lot of comfort that she would be wrong.

They approached the thirteenth tee box, the place where she'd found Orla Smith, and Clarissa found herself looking away from the tee box into the undergrowth and around. Not just to be scanning, but to stop herself from remembering the views she had before. The art world was much better. You turned up when there was a big mark on the wall where a painting had been. You didn't find dead bodies everywhere. Maybe she should go back. Maybe that's what she should do. But this team was good and kept her fresh. Clarissa threw the idea to the back of her mind, pointing over to the far side of the thirteenth and Frank drove along the edge past a large group of azaleas.

'Do you know when this is out properly, the colours are just stunning.'

'I'm sure it is, Frank,' said Clarissa, 'but I don't need a

conversation about the course at the moment. I need you to keep your eyes peeled like mine.'

'Sorry. I'm sorry. Of course.'

She moved her hand across and put it on top of his. 'It's all right. You're not used to this, but it's times like these you have to just focus. You probably don't want to think about Pádraig, what could have happened to him and where he is. I don't really want to either, but you need to focus on our task. Keep scanning. Hopefully, we might get a helicopter over soon. Be able to put a thermal image on everything. If he's out here somewhere, that would certainly bring him to our attention.'

'Well, I'll tell you something,' said the head greenkeeper, 'he's not down this side of the thirteenth. I'll route around the back of the tee box, down a little track and you'll see the par five twelfth. It's got a lake right in front of the green, it's quite stunning. There's a large birch tree, which overhangs the top half of the green, just lovely. It's secluded away from the rest of the course, beautiful hole. We worked really hard on it. I remember the initial designs, but since then we've put more colour into it and we've—'

Clarissa's hand moved across again. 'Someday I'll come back, and you can tell me all about it, Frank,' she said, 'trust me. I'd love that, but right now I need to do my job and I need you to help me with it.'

'Sorry,' said the man again. He drove down a smart stone path, turned round the corner to where Clarissa saw a large green where a flag was sat at the front with a small runoff into a pond. Even from here, she could see that there were fish inside. As the bright sunshine shone across the surface, she looked down the long fairway, some tough bunkers on either side, and could see why Frank was so proud of the hole.

As they drove further right and passed the edge of the green, she took a scan back towards the far end of the green. 'Frank, stop,' said Clarissa, 'don't look.'

If there was the one thing she didn't want him to do, it was to disobey her at that point. Frank turned. The man yelled. Clarissa could understand why. There, hanging from the fabulous birch tree about three-quarters away across the green and about six feet up off it, was Pádraig O'Reilly. He was dressed as he had been in the meeting. His neck and head hanging to one side, the body swinging in the breeze.

Frank turned to her, tears pummelling from his eyes and he buried his head into her shawl. She wrapped her arms around his head holding him tight. 'Bollocks,' she said, 'bollocks.'

Chapter 21

Hope stood at the side of the twelfth green, looking over at Jona and her team as they worked on bringing down the body of Pádraig O'Reilly. She'd come out for an update, but Jona had been busy supervising and she knew better than to interrupt the woman when she was in full flow. The scene was gruesome, and Hope turned away and looked down the lavish fairway, the white sandy bunkers on either side. It looked funny, as it wasn't really the sand you got at the beach, much paler. It also seemed a long way to hit a ball. She gazed off at what she presumed was the tee box for the twelfth. Hope wasn't into golf. Sure, she had seen it on the TV, but it wasn't something she'd ever sat down and watched.

'Ironic, isn't it?' said Clarissa. Hope nearly jumped. She turned around and saw the shawl-covered woman not exactly smiling but drinking in the surroundings. *If you were going to die*, thought Hope, *this certainly was a beautiful location to do it.* The tree that they'd strung him up from was lovely in its own right, even if it did seem rather macabre in its current situation.

'Ironic?' said Hope.

'Yes, you close off the course because of all the trouble that's going on, and you leave it wide open for someone to come out here. If there had been golfers playing, it would have been much harder to do this. I'm reckoning they must have had a pull rope.'

'So, I hear,' said Hope. 'Jona will be over in a minute though.'

The word going around the clubhouse was suicide, but Hope thought there were easier ways to do that. O'Reilly was hanging so high that you could have walked Hope underneath with Macleod on her shoulders. When she looked up at the branches, she thought it was an awfully long way for a person to climb out only to hang himself.

There was more about this than a suicide. Even if O'Reilly had taken his own life, there was something being said by the location where he'd hung himself. She gave a rub of her shoulders. A chill had gone down through her. She wasn't immune to feeling it, wasn't immune to that cold feeling of despair. O'Reilly was number three, leaving yet another vacancy. It was one that would need to be filled, but who would fill it.

It worried Hope that the scramble was still going on, that despite these deaths, club business was being enacted and by people who were against what was probably going to happen.

It was another ten minutes before the body was safely put to the ground and another ten before Jona came over to Hope. She thought her friend looked disturbed. This was unusual for Jona.

'What's up?' asked Hope.

'There's something not quite right about this,' said Jona. 'I have a feeling that there's going to be more damage around the neck than a simple drop would cause. I think there are almost friction burns.'

'How do you mean?' asked Hope.

'If you put a rope around someone's neck and you just drop and neck's broken, it doesn't move that far. However, if somebody was to haul them up there, say, killed them and then put them up, because of the constant shifting and pulling, the neck would rub on the rope, you'd get much more developed marks. I think I'm seeing them, but I need to do more tests. It's just an initial observation.'

'I was thinking it's a heck of a walkout on that branch to drop yourself off as well.'

'Precisely. You'd have to be quite fit to get up there too.'

'Okay,' said Hope. 'Imagine it isn't a suicide. Imagine you've got to get him up there. How?'

'Well, I'd make sure he was dead first. Then rope around the neck. Throw that rope up and over the branch because the branch is strong enough to take the weight, pull them up, secure your rope to the ground, climb the tree, secure him via his rope to the tree and then untie your rope. Bring it back down. At the moment, that's what I think happened. We'll check for footprints around the green, but it's not going to be easy. I think we've had a blast of rain or snow through here since he's been up. Clothes are wet.'

Hope went to turn away, but Jona called after her. 'You know there's going to be another.'

'Yes,' said Hope, 'but this one can't be a killing. The tour is getting edgy. They'll be edgy enough about this, but if this is a suicide and It's linked into his disgrace that works, the tour can live with that. It's just somebody got caught with his pants down,' said Hope. 'Couldn't live with it. But if it's a killing made to look like suicide, we can see the killer's change in tactics. Carrying out the agenda but keeping the tour placated.'

'Are you missing something then?' asked Jona, 'Is somebody on the wrong side? Is somebody pretending to be on the wrong side?'

'Well, if they are, then we're safe because all they'll do is change their vote.'

'But if we're not, then something else is coming down the line.'

Hope walked back up to the clubhouse and was simply amazed at the number of press that had now arrived. It seemed like a juicy story of a man's infidelity was even more important than the murders that had been going on. Hope stopped when she saw Macleod and he indicated that they should go inside. Once inside the front door of the clubhouse, he took Hope again to one side.

'I've asked for extra uniform up here, we need to keep the cordon intact.'

'I was just down with Jona,' started Hope.

'It wasn't a criticism,' said Macleod. 'I didn't realise they would come out in their droves like they are. Anything to do with sex, anything to do with infidelity, they're all over it,' said Macleod. 'Anyway, Sergeant Halford's on it. He's extending the perimeter and will make sure that there's more bodies down and around the golf course. What's your thinking at the moment?'

'It's not a suicide, Seoras. I was talking with Jona. We reckon we know how they could have put him up there. Got to climb a tree though as well. Got to be somebody reasonably agile. Reckon he may have been dead before they put up.'

'Who are you thinking?'

'I don't know,' said Hope. 'I'm thinking it might be somebody is playing the wrong side. Somebody who's pretending to be one-sided, actually wants this tour, after all. Can't be Cecil Ayres. he's too old, isn't he? If It's Begley, he's playing a hell of a game.'

'You should probably get Ross onto that, get him into the game. Could be, maybe he's been looking at this all along.'

'Amy Johnson, she seems so driven, but she's got an alibi for that first one. Difficult for the second one as well, she was up in the clubhouse.

'So, Andrew Peters is in the hot seat, is he?' asked Macleod.

'Can't see Andrew Peters up in that branch,' said Hope. 'We're struggling. We're really struggling.'

'Maybe you should go at it from a different angle,' said Macleod.

'How do you mean?' asked Hope.

'Going to be another election, I take it. Maybe you should focus on the candidates.'

* * *

Ewan could not believe his luck. They had closed the sodden golf course. What a joy. Along with his friend Michael, the two young teenagers were racing across the green course. Everybody's attention seemed to be up on that other course but here on the open links, no one was about, no one cared that two young boys were racing here and there. They were running down through a gully that fronted one of the greens. When you stood in it, it went all the way up to your shoulders. It was like being in a trench.

Ewan popped his head up over the top, pretended to fire at some Germans on the far side, shouted, 'Achtung,' and told

Michael he needed to duck, it was incoming. Then they were off charging down the gully.

It ended in a small drop, a tiny waterfall into a relatively large lake. The other side of the lake had a river that ran out to the sea and Ewan in his wetsuit, took a leap over the gully, past the waterfall and into the lake. He felt the water go up and over his head, but his feet quickly touched down with the water maybe a foot above him. He swam up, broke the surface, turned and laughed at Michael.

'Come on, in you get,' he said, 'they're shooting at you.' Michael jumped in with a large splash, descending underneath the water. He came back up quickly flapping with his hands, yelling.

'Ah, It's my foot. Something got my foot.'

'What do you mean something got your foot? There's nothing in here, it would just be the bottom, it'll be a rock or something.'

'No, something hit my foot. I'm telling you, something's down there.'

Ewan laughed. Michael was a great friend, but he was an idiot, the number of things he complained about, the number of things that got in his way.

'Stay here,' said Ewan. He duck-dived down to the bottom and started feeling around. There were rocks and pebbles, and he worked his way along. Surely, he must have been where Michael had come up. His breath was running out, so he rose to the surface, checked his bearings. Yes, nearly. He took a breath and went back down again. His hands crawled around the bottom, little bits of green algae covering some of the rocks that felt so slippery in his hands, but then there was something else, something metallic. Something which cut into his hand, not deep, but a slice. His other hand swung over and hit what felt like the hilt of a knife. He grabbed it and rose to the surface.

'Look at this. Look at this,' said Ewan.

Michael was now out of the water, sitting on the edge, looking over at him. 'You're bleeding,' he said.

Ewan looked at his hand. There was a bit of blood running out, but nothing to worry about. He turned the thin blade over in his hand noting the decorative hilt. 'I'm going to take this home,' he said.

'No,' said Michael, 'you need to take that somewhere. We can't take stuff away at the moment. Lots of bad things going on at the golf club. There's been murders up there.'

'And you think this is a murder weapon? Don't be ridiculous.'

Ewan propped the knife at the edge of the water, jumped out. 'I need to have a look at this cut though,' he said, 'come on, let's head home.'

'I'll need a bandage around my fingers.'

* * *

Jona entered the incident room in the clubhouse looking somewhat puffed. She glanced across at Hope with eyes that said, 'This better be worth it,' before walking over towards Ross. In front of Ross, in a clear plastic bag on the table was a knife with an ornate handle. The blade was thin, and Jona bent down to examine it closely. She turned the bag over before quickly looking around the room and putting some gloves on. She removed the plastic bag and started turning the knife over and over in her hand.

'And where did you get this?' asked Jona.

'Newtonmoray police station,' said Ross. 'Two kids dropped

it in. Apparently, they were on . . .' he looked down at a map of the golf courses, 'the fifteenth on the links course. There's a little lake at the side of one of the greens. They were mucking about, swimming in it. Managed to find that, one of them cut himself, and took it home. Their mum saw them bandaging themselves up, asked what had happened. She saw the knife and brought it into the police station.'

'A good job she did,' said Jona. 'I can't say one hundred percent but this . . . this is a serious possibility for that first murder. Not the second, definitely not the second, but the first one, this knife is a possibility. I'll get on it and find out if it definitely is but if I was you, I'd work on the premise it is.'

'What do you know about the decoration on the handle?' asked Ross.

'Nothing at the moment.' said Jona.

'I'll look into it,' said Ross. 'See if I can find out what type of knife it is as well.'

'Good,' said Hope, 'are you having a coffee, Jona.'

'No, I've just legged it all the way up here and I've got to leg it back out. We're not finished down there, but we're not finding much. What I can tell you is that neck was broken before he was put up. It's not a suicide.'

'Keep that quiet,' said Hope, 'within the team, I mean. That doesn't go anywhere else. I don't want the killer thinking that their plans are going awry. See if we can weed them out.'

She turned and looked across the room where Macleod was staring out of the window. He hadn't come over to see the knife when it had been brought in. He simply stood in the corner, but he was listening because Seoras was always listening. He was keeping out of her way; she knew that.

'I'll run you down in a buggy,' said Ross. Jona thanked him

and the two left the room. Hope went to approach Macleod, but Clarissa grabbed her shoulder.

'With what's going on, I think I need to go and see these two anti-tour candidates who are standing for the next position.'

'Good idea,' said Hope.

'I'm just going to go over them with the ground staff, see what they know about them,' said Clarissa.

'Spending a lot of time with the ground staff,' said Macleod without even looking around.

'Well, they hear things,' said Clarissa, and turned to walk out.

'Nice man,' said Macleod. Hope watched Clarissa turn back again, pointing a finger at Macleod, looking at Hope, and mouthing the words, 'I'm gonna kill him' before she made her way out of the room.

'You don't miss much, do you?' said Hope.

'Try not to,' he said.

'We're getting tight here, aren't we, though? We're getting tight. Everything's coming to a head. They're going to vote this tour in soon. It's ramping it up. It's going to force the killer to act.'

'That's true,' said Macleod. 'Accurate.'

'How did you cope with it?' said Hope suddenly. 'How do you sit here sending the rest of us out.'

'Because I think through things,' said Macleod, 'but that's me. You've got to cope how you cope,' he said, suddenly turning around. 'You're in the hot seat, Hope. You do what you do. If that means you've got to put some leg work in, do some leg work. I'm an old fart. I can't walk that far all day. Time pressure is just time pressure. Think what you can do. Make it useful. Anything else I can do for you at the moment?'

'No,' said Hope. 'Clarissa and I will take care of these new candidates. Maybe that's where we need to be.'

Chapter 22

I t had started snowing by the time Clarissa got back over to the incident room in the clubhouse. She marched in, looked around, and then walked directly over to Hope.

'Seoras is not here, then? Don't have to watch out for any more quips, do I?'

'No,' said Hope suddenly. 'What's the deal?'

'Well, Frank says that these two new candidates on the anti-tour side are an Angela Downes, a middle-aged mother, and a Daniel MacIver. He's in his seventies. He's deaf as well. Seems that he's been at the club for a while. Goes out on his little buggy to play, doesn't want a lot of change, never seems to play the new course.

'Angela Downes, however, is slightly different. She's up here occasionally. She does like the new course but she's also very wary of things becoming expensive, outside people coming in. She's been quite vocal about making the focus on club members rather an occasional players. More to do with the average golfer. Certainly not the model they're talking about with corporate businesses. I would say she'd be quite a challenge by the sounds of it. Frank says she's very strongly opinionated.'

'Daniel would be an easier target. How are they in terms of popularity?'

'Angela is probably the best. She's well-liked amongst the ladies. She's probably the main threat. According to Frank, the two pro candidates, one of them Jasper Mullins, is only a slip of a lad, less than twenty. He'll not get many votes according to Frank. Deirdre Monroe, however, she'll be reasonably popular as a former lady's captain. But Frank seems to think that Angela Downes would take the vote over Deirdre any day.'

'Right then, so we come at this from the point of view that they're probably going to be potential victims. We'll need to protect them. You go visit Angela Downes,' said Hope. 'See what she has to say for herself. Get her some protection as well. Also, I'll go see Daniel MacIver, make sure he's got protection. Although by the signs of it, it's really between the two women.'

'Changed times at a golf club,' said Clarissa. 'I still remember the day I kicked the vice chairman of one of the clubs. Serious boot just under the knee and then bounced him off the lockers.'

Hope looked slightly shocked. 'Why?' she asked.

'He wanted to make it so the ladies were only able to play during the week. Wanted all the tee boxes to be available for the men only. I think he called me a surly bitch. I overheard him. He thought he was okay because he was in the men's locker rooms. He was quite surprised when I tapped him on the shoulder.'

'I'm sure he was. What were you doing in the men's locker rooms?'

'Coming to deliver him a message. He was stood in a towel as well,' laughed Clarissa. 'He turned round, one hand on this towel, and just lit on me. Last time he lit on me though; teed off that weekend, I did. Half past nine. That's the slot he used to go out in.'

Hope shook her head. The image of Clarissa attacking a man in a towel was not one that seemed unbelievable but also wasn't one she wanted to countenance for too long. 'Go find Angela Downs, then call me.'

As Clarissa left the room, Hope chided herself. 'Time to go,' she said. 'Time to go and do. Let's go see Daniel MacIver.' She looked over at Ross, deeply focused on his computer, and the various other constables littered about the room. 'On my mobile, if you need me,' said Hope.

'Of course,' said Ross, not even looking up.

* * *

Angela Downes lived on the edge of Inverness, a reasonable distance from Newtonmoray Golf Club, which told Clarissa that the woman must have been a real golfer because there were courses closer. She was someone who travelled for the course. Well, it may have been for the ambience and the liveliness of the clubhouse, but Clarissa thought not in this case. This woman would be a real golfer.

She knocked on the door of a newly built four-bedroom house with a green door standing out in front of the pale red brick. It was opened by a woman who stood slightly taller than Clarissa with a countenance that she shouldn't be messed with.

'Detective Sergeant Clarissa Urquhart. I'm looking for Angela Downs, please.'

'I'm Angela,' said the woman. 'What's this about?'

'I believe you're standing in the election at the Newtonmoray Golf Club.'

'You better come in,' said Angela, who stood back from the door, leaving it open for Clarissa to walk in. 'You best go into the left,' she said. 'I think one of the seats is free.'

Clarissa opened the door into a lounge area and found it looking clean but in a current state of disarray. There were toys here and there, a train track with a choo-choo running along it, and at least two kids on the ground rolling around with soft toys.

'Sorry,' she said. 'He's got the kids at home at the moment. Not mine, of course. My son's.'

Clarissa had thought it strange when she looked at the woman. She was a wee bit older than what she thought was a reasonable childbearing age. Never having had kids, Clarissa didn't like to judge.

'Do you want a cup of tea or anything?'

'You've got your hands full,' said Clarissa. 'No, I just wanted to chat. If you're standing in this election and given what's going on at the club, we need to get you some protection.'

'That won't be necessary,' said the woman. 'I mean, it's a bit of a shock Pádraig hanging himself, but he was up to no good, wasn't he? I mean him and Orla. Well, it's no wonder he feels guilty about that.'

'Why?' asked Clarissa.

'Have you met his wife? Lovely woman. Really, really lovely woman. Don't know how she stood for him if I'm honest. Pádraig was a bit of a boy. I didn't know anything about the affair but he spoke his mind, a good golfer but see, once he had a few drinks inside him. Bit of a shock about Orla, though. She was a quiet one. That's what they say though, isn't it sometimes? Quiet ones, under the covers they're the wild ones.'

Clarissa wasn't quite sure how to take that and thought the conversation was getting away from her. 'I really insist that you have some protection. There's been two murders and a suicide we're investigating. The first two murders could potentially be to do with the board and the situation with the tour.'

'That damn tour has nothing for me,' said Angela. 'Think about all the tourists. Don't want those people coming in their big corporate boxes. I mean, if they had pushed the links to bring something like the Open here, or even the Scottish Open. Wow, that would've been something. On the links, you know, it'd be a bit more traditional. Not this target golf up in the other course. It is target golf. It all looks beautiful, but, you know, ball in the air bypasses everything on the ground. Even an old duffer like me can get around.'

'What did you play off?' asked Clarissa.

'Five,' said Angela Downes, which caused Clarissa to raise her eyebrows.

Clarissa had managed to get down to a twelve handicap once when she played, and was what she felt was a respectable handicap, but this woman was clearly a very good player.

'Your protection's going to be unnecessary though.'

'Why is that?'

'I'm dropping out. I mean, look at me. Maybe I was just being daft. My son and his wife, they both work. I've got to look after these kids more and then they'll be wanting their board meetings, and they don't do board meetings like they used to in the evening all the time. No. They've got to be in during the day. It's not really what I want.'

'Do you work?' asked Clarissa.

'No, my husband works.'

'Is he not worried about you standing with all that's going on.'

'Of course, he is. He said to me, 'Don't do it.' He said he didn't like what was happening. But you don't get scared off by things like that. You got to live your life. You've got to go and do, haven't you?'

'Normally I'd say yes,' answered Clarissa. 'But to be honest, if there's somebody running around killing people, that tends to make me rethink how I see the world.'

'You're like him,' she said. 'Very dry sense of humour. Anyway, he's delighted I'm not standing.'

'Good,' said Clarissa.

'Are you sure I can't get you a coffee?'

'Go on then,' said Clarissa and watched Angela leave the room. Clarissa stood up, stepped across to an array of photographs that were on the wall. She looked at the different kids. They were two young girls, almost babies in one of them. And she saw another one. Three. A boy followed by another boy. At least she assumed they were boys. What colours were the boys. Did they still put babies in colours?

Clarissa wouldn't have been happy putting them in colours if she had been a mum. She'd put them in tartan. That would suit them. Urquhart tartan. She grinned, then felt a little hollow. She didn't have any of that. She'd grown up, her life racing around here and there, and yes, she'd lived a supposed high life. There'd been plenty of guys, never any particularly serious. Then she'd come down to the art squad. A little bit of high life with the wine and everything else that went with that. Kids just never seemed to be a part of what she wanted to do. She never settled down. She almost did once.

Clarissa thought about Bernard. It was such a dull name.

That was the case in life sometimes. People who were exciting, people who made you think, made you excited, quite often they were clothed in the most boring names or outfits. Bernard always wore a tweed suit, but the man could talk about art. Not in that showy way, but he really understood.

She'd been terribly disappointed when he suddenly left to go to Austria. They'd been seeing each other for, maybe, six months. She thought he might have asked her to move in. There wasn't going to be a ring involved. He wasn't that sort of a person. But he'd gone off to Austria and died in a skiing accident. Sometimes you look back and think life was cruel. She could have had kids with Bernard. He'd have been a good dad.

Angela Downes returned with a coffee snapping Clarissa out of her trance at one of the pictures.

'Four grandkids,' she said.

'Yes. All my son's. That's Jessica and that's Lynn and there's Jake and that is Timmy. That's Jessica and Orla on the floor.'

Clarissa looked down at the two girls rolling about. *One was nearly five*, she thought, *and seems to be desperately playing with the other*.

'Jake's not here, and Timmy's asleep upstairs.'

'Excellent. I take it Timmy's the baby.'

'Yeah, Jake's three but he's away at the moment,' said Angela. She seemed to stare out of the window. Clarissa thought she looked nervous.

'Where is he?'

'He's stopping on with the other side of the family.'

Clarissa nodded. She sat down and continued the conversation with Angela. It turned mainly to the golf and the courses. There was little point to the conversation, for the woman wasn't standing and was in the clear. Clarissa was only being polite by finishing her coffee. She handed it to Angela who disappeared into the kitchen. Jessica came up to her. 'Are you going to find Jake?'

'Jake's with your other granny.'

'Don't be silly,' said the girl. 'Other granny lives miles away. Are you going to find him? He hasn't been here. He came with us.'

Angela walked into the front room.

'I think Jessica's a little bit confused,' said Clarissa. 'She's looking for Jake. Says he was here.'

'He was here the other day. He's gone away. I've told Jessica. He's had to go away. That's the trouble at that age. They don't understand, do they? I've taken up enough of your time,' said Angela. 'I'm sorry. I need to get on. Washing to do. Timmy will be up in a minute.'

Clarissa stood up and offered her hand. 'Of course, but thank you for that and take care. It's good to see you off the danger line.'

'It does feel a lot better,' she told Clarissa. Clarissa walked down the path to her car and when she got inside, she glanced over towards the house. She could have sworn the woman was looking out of the blinds at her. Something didn't feel right in Clarissa's gut.

Chapter 23

Hope marched back into the incident room, flung her jacket onto her seat and hit the table with her hand. 'What next?' she said to herself. 'What next?' It was then she realised that Macleod was across the room with Ross.

'That's all the briefings on the table?' she said quickly.

'Yes,' said Ross. 'I've gone through the four candidates. To be honest, the pro campaigners, Jasper Mullins and Deirdre Monroe, they just look like normal people. There's nothing in there to say that they're a killer.'

'There's nothing anywhere to say anyone's a killer. This is the problem,' said Hope suddenly. 'Got to be something. There's got to be something.'

'What's wrong?' asked Macleod.

'What's wrong is Angela Downs has pulled out of the race. Clarissa just called me. What's also wrong is I went to see Daniel MacIver. He is in his seventies. He is deaf. There's no way that old man is actually going to win this. They're not going to bother killing him. Angela was the forerunner. Deirdre Monroe's going to win it now. Deirdre Monroe's going to come in. That's going to give them five.'

'No, it's not,' said Macleod. 'You've got Peters, you've got

Amy Johnson. You've got Jim Durbin. If you get this Deirdre Monroe, that's only four. Still a vacancy at Padraig's.'

'No, they need a decision. They're going to take two from this. They're going to have temporary board members in, so they can vote. They've passed that previously; that changes things. They use this vote; they bring those two in. Suddenly you've got five versus two and it's done. The killer doesn't have to react anymore. Daniel MacIver is a nobody. That's what I found out when I went. He's a nobody. He doesn't even think he's going to get a couple of votes. He's standing on principle. I think the only reason he stayed in was because he knew he wasn't going to get any votes. Angela Downs was going to take all that the anti-tour vote.'

Hope turned and kicked a chair. It disappointingly bounced only a foot away.

'You were going to beat them,' said Macleod. 'Pull a trap.'

'Yes,' said Hope, 'but now that's unworkable.'

Jona marched into the room with a smile on her face. 'I can confirm that the knife found by the boys killed Sandy Mackintosh. I haven't got much history on it. It's possibly Spanish.'

'Very definitely Spanish. Used in a former martial art back in the Middle Ages. I've got some more detail on that, Jona,' announced Ross.

'But I,' replied Jona, 'can confirm the blade fits the wounds. Quite a mean blade too. Proper weapon.'

'But definitely not what happened on the second one,' said Macleod.

'No, not at all.'

'What was the point of that, then? Do you think they're trying to confuse us?' said Hope. 'If you look at it, we've got two murders. There are differences in them, different weapons used. We then have us a suicide.'

'We don't have a suicide,' said Jona. 'I can confirm his neck was broken before he was hoisted up there. The marks on his neck show where a rope was used to pull him up before a different rope was hung around his neck and he was allowed to drop. However, at that point he was dead.'

'He was dead?' said Hope. 'So, what was the killer's point? Somebody leaked the scandal. Have we found out who leaked that scandal?'

'No,' said Ross. 'The press said the documents arrived. Nobody delivered them but arrived in the post. No marks on them. Arrived to a lot of the local newspapers and it all blew up from there.'

'So, the killer's tried to push him into committing suicide. She's exposed him and then when he hasn't, the killer has decided to make an example. Or did the killer all along intend to just make it look like suicide?'

'They're under pressure from the tour,' said Macleod. 'They have to . . .'

'What are they going to do this time, Seoras? They don't need to do anything. I've got no angle here. I have got no angle, Seoras. It's got to be Peters, hasn't it? It's got to be Peters.'

'No, it doesn't,' said Macleod. 'It doesn't have to be Peters. We've got nothing definite. Don't clutch at straws. Don't go after something because you don't have a gut feel on this.'

'No, I don't,' said Hope, 'and that's the problem. I don't have a gut feel.'

She marched off towards the window and the silence behind her just grew. Hope was aware of everyone staring and then she heard the feet of Macleod coming over. It was Seoras's walk. Ross was more military-like, quick clipping steps. Jona was lighter on the foot.

'Process,' said Macleod in her ear. 'Process. You said to me Peters couldn't have got up that tree.'

'He couldn't,' said Hope, 'but Johnson, she's got an alibi for the first one. The second one, maybe she . . .' Hope stopped all of a sudden. 'The locker,' she said. 'The locker. When we toured her locker, she had kit in it from the gym.'

'Did it?' said Macleod.

'It did. The kit was wet and I thought the kit's wet because she's been to the gym that morning. She's fit, really fit. If somebody knew about Orla Smith and Padraig, they could have . . .'

'Used that. Put Orla in the same place,' said Macleod.

'Tell her a time to be there. Tell her to . . .'

'Yes,' said Macleod. 'Who's got most to lose from all of this?'

'But she's got that alibi. She's got that alibi for the first one. She's at the club. Jona,' said Hope suddenly, turning around and staring at the Asian woman. 'are you sure about the time of death? Sandy Mackintosh?'

'Are you questioning . . .?'

'Don't,' said Hope. 'Just answer the question. Are you sure of the time of death?'

'Yes, I am,' she said.

Hope raised a fist. 'It's there, Seoras. It's there. What is it?'

'You'll get there,' he said quietly. 'You'll get there. Just get there soon. Assistant Chief Constable's been on to me. He wants a result in this. The press, well, you know how it is once the press gets involved; suddenly everybody gets interested.'

'Do we have any answer from the board about when they're going to run this election?' asked Hope.

'Called a hasty meeting for tonight. They want the board meeting in the morning. It seems the press is getting to them, too,' said Ross.

'Tonight? Tomorrow morning. Need more time,' said Hope. 'We need more time.' She stared around the room. 'They're not going to act, Seoras. Not against Daniel MacIver. I really don't see where to go with this. How do I drag them out? How do I?'

'You've got a theory. You need to test your theory. If someone knew about the affair between O'Reilly and Orla Smith, and that person was using that to coerce Orla Smith out, they would also need to get from where they were down to there and back to still be seen in a building. Is there time to do it?'

'Jona,' said Hope. 'Go out to the thirteenth.'

'We finished the thirteenth before. We've been around it all. I've dug up everything. There's nothing there. There's no . . .'

'Go to the thirteenth.'

Jona flashed her eyes over at Macleod.

'She's the boss,' said Macleod, stepping back.

'It's blooming starting to snow out there.'

'Thirteenth, Jona. Now, please. How long is it going to take you to get there?'

'Give me fifteen minutes. What am I meant to do when I'm out there?'

'Just stay there. Stay there and pretend you're looking for someone. Pretend you're meeting someone so you're on the lookout for them.'

'Okay,' she said.

Macleod sat down on a seat. 'Ross, give me those files you were talking about. I need to read through these again. Check through these candidates for tonight. Also, give me the profiles of everyone else. The board and that.'

'You think I'm wrong in this?' said Hope. 'You're just going to sit down?'

'This is your theory. Go and test it. Me? I've got other things to get on with. What do you want me to do, run down with you? Kind of going to kill the experiment.'

Hope nearly burst out laughing. The idea of Macleod running down across the golf course to sneak up on someone, because that's what she was going to do. Could Amy Johnson get out there? Could Amy Johnson manage to sneak up on someone and then get back? She was strong enough to haul O'Reilly up in the air. She worked out at the gym. When you saw her in her smart outfits, you did think of her as a resourceful woman, but not strong and capable of handling lots of the physical side. She sold herself as the eye candy, but she was more than that, thought Hope.

Hope had a set of clothes for the gym stowed in her car for those opportune moments when she could escape a case. She went to change and soon was in shorts and a T-shirt in the incident room. She sent Ross outside to make sure Amy Johnson wasn't hanging about and then asked Macleod how long Jona had been gone.

'Fifteen minutes, twenty seconds. You should be away by now,' he said calmly.

Hope bolted out of the room, down the stairs, and out of the back of the clubhouse. She made for the shortest distance into the undergrowth. No one saw her, and soon she was running through vegetation, knee deep at times, lifting her legs up high, pushing herself on. The snow was falling quite thickly now, but she ignored that, her red ponytail bobbing around behind her, hitting her on the shoulder with every foot that struck the ground. She pushed hard.

Soon, she arrived close to the thirteenth tee box and could make Jona out through the undergrowth. The Asian woman was looking this way and that and Hope snuck along carefully until she was almost within touching distance of her. As Jona looked the other way, Hope struck.

Clearing the bushes, she stuck her hand up to Jona's throat. 'You've just been killed through the throat. I drag you over, bend you, leave you on the golf bag. That's here.'

'Where's the golf bag come from?' said Jona.

'Left out earlier, so we drag it from over here, put it in. You're now set up. I'm gone. Walk yourself back when you're ready.'

Hope took off back into the undergrowth. Her lungs were burning, but she drove herself as hard as she could. Soon she was back at the clubhouse, running the short distance in, back up the stairs, and collapsed into the incident room.

'How'd it go?' asked Macleod, without looking up.

'Jona's dead. Golf bag must have been out there.'

'Jona's dead?' said Ross suddenly.

Macleod waved his hand in the air. 'Not like that, Ross. Under fifteen minutes,' said Macleod. 'She may be fitter than you.'

Hope was bent double, breathing heavily. 'Like hell she's fitter than me,' she spat.

There was a knock at the door and a constable marched in. He stared at Hope as she turned round, trying to lift herself to her full height to look like the leading investigator she was meant to be.

'What?' she said. The young man stared at her, then caught himself. 'Sergeant Halford is asking if you want extra people out tonight.'

'Yes,' said Hope. 'Tell him to do that but keep it low-key. I don't think anything's going to happen at the meeting. Keep the protection on Daniel MacIver also.'

The constable nodded, took one last look at Hope, and walked out. Hope shot a glance to Macleod.

'What is it with you men when women are exercising?'

'You don't get to ask me questions like that. I'm your superior officer.'

'More like he doesn't want to answer that question,' said Ross. Macleod put his hand up, giving a waving tut to Ross.

'Theory fits, Seoras, theory fits. But she still wasn't there for the first one. She was in the gym. How does that work? What are we missing with that? More importantly, how do I trap her? Because this is circumstantial. There's no evidence. There's no . . .'

'It'll come,' said Macleod. 'You need to trust the team. It'll come. Keep your eye on events tonight. Watch for it.'

'Easy for you to say. What should I do now? How do I force that to happen?'

'You don't,' said Macleod. 'What you should do now is shower.'

Hope gave him a long stare. 'That's the best you've got.'

'For now,' said Macleod.

Chapter 24

Hope stood at the window of the incident room in the clubhouse, looking down at the golf membership filing into the hall on the floor below. She would step down soon to have a look at the meeting, but she was awaiting an update from Sergeant Halford as to the status of Daniel MacIver and whether he had arrived. Her query was soon answered as she saw an elderly man hobbling in surrounded by four police constables. She gave a sigh and walked down the steps of the clubhouse to the hall below. She stood at the back and watched as the meeting got into full swing with Andrew Peters at the front announcing the process for voting. All three candidates were allowed to speak, and she thought Daniel MacIver was a rambling mess.

He wasn't making any sense. When Peters explained that the vote would then bring two members on Board and not just the one, albeit in temporary capacities, there was little dissension from the membership. Peters said that they had a decision to make about the tour. He spoke eloquently about why they had to do it now, why there was such pressure on with so many press around. He explained that if they made the decision, the press would go away once all this hoo-ha about O'Reilly had died down. The scandal would be over and in two years' time or so, there would be a tour event at the club providing the Board were happy to go ahead. Cecil Ayers stood up, pointing out that he disagreed with bringing the tour here, but he was in full favour of what was happening.

Hope watched as the meeting continued. The vote took place, and Andrew Peters announced that Jasper Mullins and Deidre Monroe would join the Board. The membership were advised that a Board meeting would be taking place the next morning. Hope watched as everyone filed out, including a rather depressed Cecil Ayers. He was grabbed by Begley on the way out.

'This is it,' said Begley. 'This is the end of the club as we know it. A corporate hellhole is what it's going to turn into. You can say goodbye to all the good nights in here. You could say goodbye to our bars, our restaurant. It'll all be done for these people coming in. We've lost, Cecil. We've lost.'

Ayers looked like he was about to cry. Peters departed the room accompanied by Amy Johnson, telling him to go and get a good night's sleep before the meeting the next day. She said she would advise the tour of what had happened and would tell them they expect a decision by lunchtime the next day. The woman was in a jovial mood, and Hope watched her like a hawk.

'Off to celebrate,' said Hope.

'No. Off to home. My life doesn't fully revolve around here,' said Amy.

She was dressed in a skirt that came just above the knees, heels, a blouse with a jacket. Hope could swear that Peters was enjoying the view as they left. She felt frustrated, angry. Ross was upstairs, still trying, still poring through his CCTV, still looking at all their angles. Macleod hadn't bothered to come down. When she'd left, he was sitting, going through the briefing packs of Ross, and she heard him pick up the phone and asked for Jona.

As for her sergeant, she had no idea where Clarissa was. She had disappeared most of the afternoon, but in truth, Hope had nothing for her. She had nowhere to put her, nothing to find out, and she wasn't going to take Halford's sense of responsibility away from him by attaching Clarissa to look after Daniel MacIver. She found it difficult to not swear as she made her way back up to the room above.

'I take it from your face that they both got in,' asked Ross.

'Yes', she said. 'Where's Seoras?'

'Said he'd be done for tonight. Jane was expecting him.'

'I think we're stuffed on this one, Ross. I think we're stuffed on this one.'

'That's not what the boss said.'

'Where's Clarissa anyway?'

'Last I heard, which was quite a while ago, she was off with that guy Frank from the grounds team. She was going out to scout around the course.'

'Well, I suppose why not?'

'I haven't heard back from her though.'

'It'd be nice if she kept in touch.' On cue, Hope's mobile began to vibrate. She looked at the caller and pressed the button. 'Where the hell are you been?' she asked Clarissa.

'There's going to be a golf cart coming for you. Frank will be driving. Get on it. He'll take you to me, somewhere important, and I could do with a little bit of help.'

'What do you mean a little bit of help?'

'Just come quietly. Don't make a fuss. Don't want anyone

up there to get spooked.'

'What do you mean spooked?'

'Take it the meeting's over? If so, Frank should be about.'

The call was closed down. Hope stood for a moment, wondering what the heck was going on. She walked over and took her jacket off the coat hook, put it on and went to leave.

'Is that you for the night, boss?' asked Ross.

'No, but if anybody else comes in not from the team, tell them yes.'

'Where are you off?' he asked.

'I don't know,' she said. 'I don't know.'

Hope walked down the stairs of the golf club through the entrance lobby, stepped outside and looked left and right. He would be somewhere, she thought, if Clarissa had organised it. There in the dark, about fifty metres away, was a little golf cart with Frank, the head groundskeeper, in it. He motioned at her to come over quietly.

Hope walked, looking around her and could see no one. Everyone had gone seemingly. She climbed in beside him. Almost immediately, he put the foot down in the electric cart and drove away with a slight clink. He drove up to the new course heading down one of the paths at the rear of it.

'Where am I going?' asked Hope.

'To meet Sergeant Urquhart,' the man said quietly. 'But let's not make a lot of noise. She's occupied at the moment.

'Occupied with what?' Hope asked.

'We swept the course today, quietly. Too many people around, Clarissa said.'

Hope realised he'd called her Clarissa, but she ignored that gem of information and instead pondered on why they were searching the course.

'Clarissa spoke to Angela Downes today. Angela said she was dropping out of the race.'

'Yes,' said Hope, 'she told me that.'

'Clarissa's not stupid, though. One of the grandchildren asked Clarissa was she going to look for her brother. Clarissa only saw three grandkids in the house. Angela said that the other one was off on a trip. That's not true. I called Angela, asked if she was coming in for the meeting just on the quiet. She said her son had dropped the kids and they had to stay longer. I know her son. It's not the case. I phoned him and he said that she'd asked for the kids to stay on longer, all of them. This didn't add up, so I told Clarissa and she said that we should sweep the course.'

The buggy drove into the night and Hope looked at the white on the ground around them. Although it was coming close to spring, the weather in the highlands was such that you got snow at this time. Sometimes a week of sharp weather followed by warm weather. She hoped that next week would be warmer.

'I'm going to park up,' said Frank, 'at the end of the fifth; walk down the side, between the fifth green and the sixth tee where into the left is a little shed. It won't be that warm in there, but it has a little gasoline stove that runs. We don't use it anymore. Been locked up for a while, but you can get the key quite easily. Wouldn't be difficult to copy it. The actual key is still hanging back up, yet when we got there, it felt like there was some sort of heat from inside. We think the heater has been burning intermittently. Someone's been popping out here.'

The buggy came to a halt and Hope stepped off as advised,

walked down the side of the fifth, her feet crunching through some of the fresh snow. As she reached the end of what was a short par three, she could barely make out the hut stowed away in some trees. She came close up to it, looking around her, and tapped the door. Fortunately, because of the trees, there was not a great snowfall and she believed that she left next to no easily identifiable footprints.

There was no sign from inside, so Hope knocked again. When there was still no reply, Hope said quietly, 'This is Hope McGrath.'

'Hope, off to the left of the front door, you'll see a little gnome. Underneath, there's a key.'

Hope turned and saw sitting on a tuft of grass a little stone gnome. It had seen better days. She tipped it back and sure enough underneath was a key. Hope opened the lock and then the door and found Clarissa sitting inside. She was wrapped up tight, had a blanket around her as well as a shawl. She looked cold.

'What's going on?' asked Hope.

'Angela Downes had one of her grandchildren taken. That's why she dropped out of the race. She doesn't know where the person took the grandkid. She knows who it was, but she wouldn't say. Grandkid was in here. Frank has the child, safe and warm. I needed you to come down to give me some backup. The vote's over. The child will be returned soon.'

'Could be here all night though,' said Hope.

'Unlikely,' said Clarissa., 'They'll come now, the meeting's over, they'll get back home, whatever. They can't be seen to be staying in case anything went wrong. This hole has a different road into it. They'll come from that side. I need you in the undergrowth. If they come in to see me, you can trap them off at the door. Frank's good,' said Clarissa, 'but this is a murderer we're talking about. Needs you and me. I don't want to bring anybody else down. Too many people and we get spotted and then we don't have them. As far as I understand it, we don't have the evidence at the moment if they do make a run to not grab them.'

'Good work,' said Hope, thinking about how she was nearly ready to kill Clarissa an hour ago. 'I'll lock up. Try and stay warm.'

Hope locked up, put the key away underneath the gnome, and then hid behind a tree at least twenty metres away. She sat wrapped up in her jacket hoping that the person would come sooner rather than later. She undid her hair, letting the ponytail lie out, her hair covering her neck in attempt to stay warm. Frank could've told her to bring a big coat.

Fortunately, it was only half an hour later and Hope heard the footsteps. A short figure appeared, took a key out of its pocket, and started undoing the lock. Once it was undone, the door opened, Hope saw the person shine a light inside, there was a cry and a yell, but as they turned, Hope was already up from behind the tree. They went to run, but she threw herself forward in a rugby tackle, hitting the figure on the side and they fell down. Hope pressed down on top of the figure, but found that they lashed out, catching her with the back of their hand.

She took the blow to the chin and pushed down before another figure fell on top of the pair of them. Clarissa was down on her knees now and had grabbed the elusive figure's arm, driving it up behind their back. Hope helped her spin the figure over and handcuffed them by the wrists at the rear. Quickly, the two of them made the figure stand up.

Hope could see the smaller height of the woman and knew who it was, but she shone the torch in her face anyway. Amy Johnson stared at her.

'Got you,' said Hope. 'Bloody well got you.' She heard Clarissa make a phone call followed by a second one. The first was to Frank who turned up on a groundstaff buggy five minutes later. The second was to Sergeant Halford, and a group of six constables who arrived with him to take Amy Johnson into custody.

'You can't do me for it. I was at the gym. Everyone saw me.'

'We'll do you for child kidnap,' said Hope. 'We'll do you for blackmail. There's plenty you'll get done for.'

As the group of constables led Amy away, Clarissa offered Hope a ride on the buggy between her and Frank.

'I'm going to walk up,' she said. 'You two go on ahead. I need your report in tonight though,' she said to Clarissa.

'I'll be back up to the room in an hour or two,' she said. 'You can tell Ross what's happened.'

As the buggy disappeared, Sergeant Halford was out of sight with his constables. Hope began to trudge back towards the clubhouse. There was a chill in the air. She let her hair stay sprayed out for she was happy. Happy her team had come through, but in truth, she thought herself lucky.

More than that, she was struggling. Struggling to understand what had happened with the first murder. Amy Johnson had been seen at the gym. Had she been able to alter something around the time of death? Jona would have to go back and look at it again. Or had Jona got it wrong. She didn't get much wrong. Hope picked up the phone as she walked.

'Hope, it's John. What time of the morning is it?'

'I'm coming home,' she said. 'I'm coming home.'

'Have you wrapped it? You sound like you've wrapped it.'

'Almost,' said Hope. 'Enough to come home anyway.' She thought of her bed. She thought of the warmth of John's arms around her, but up in that head of hers, the questions were still ticking.

Chapter 25

Macleod strode into the golf club lobby and gave a nod to the constable on duty. He then climbed the stairs and made for the incident room that had been set up. Despite the case being effectively solved, the room was still reasonably busy, albeit with a very different air. As Macleod entered, he saw Clarissa laughing with Ross about something while Hope was sitting behind her desk signing off various bits of paper. There was a smile on her face, and as she stood, he saw her in a brown top that he didn't recognise.

'In good spirits today?' he asked.

'Of course, aren't you?'

'New top as well.'

'Seoras, I didn't think you cared.'

'It looks good. I could never buy anything for Jane. John's obviously got better taste.' Hope gave a smile.

'I'm still confused though,' she said. 'We've got Amy Johnson for the child kidnap. We raided her house, and we found the rope that she used to haul Pádraig O'Reilly up onto the tree. We found the knife as well that she used to kill Orla Smith. I think she was holding them in case she needed to frame another member. I think Peters was going to be in line for it if it came to it. She must have thrown away that other knife, but it's going to be hard to trace it to her. Still, at least we've got her for a couple of murders and for the child kidnap as well.

'You've done well,' said Macleod suddenly, 'really well, but it's not over.'

'What do you mean,' asked Hope, 'it's not over? Just because I can't work out how she managed that first one. Jona must have made a mistake. There's something in the science that mustn't fit.'

'No,' said Macleod. 'Did they have their board meeting this morning?'

'Well, Amy Johnson couldn't attend. I think they could strictly vote, but as I understand it, they've decided not to go ahead with the tour. When this all comes out into the public domain, she'll have murdered to bring the tour here. I don't think the tour is going to want that,' said Hope, 'and I don't think the golf club wants that stigma either. I mean, what are you going to call the tournament? The bloody eighteen? 'Oh look, here he is, heading into the twelfth with that lovely overhanging tree that the man was swinging from.' It's going to take a while for the stigma to die down.

'True,' said Macleod. 'By the way, that knife, Navaja.'

'Come again,' said Hope.

'It's Spanish. An old knife that was used as a martial art of sorts, a long time ago. Well, not that long. Although the art form's died out in a lot of ways, some people still learn it.'

'What? So, Amy Johnson used to do that as well?'

'No,' said Macleod, 'Amy Johnson was certainly the bad egg here. Amy Johnson would've taken to any lengths because she wanted a position on the tour fringes. She would've got a job that would've put her up into the big ranks, and from there, who knows. She was a woman who just didn't care how things were done. She even slept with Dermot McKinley. Picked her targets, you see—the man's lonely. Not that that makes me think any better of what he did.'

'But I don't understand,' said Hope. 'What are you saying about the first killing?'

'Are they still in the boardroom?' asked Macleod.

'I think some of them are.'

'Then come with me.' Macleod walked downstairs to the boardroom with Hope following. He knocked on the door. When he opened it, Cecil Ayres and Andrew Peters were still there.

'Good morning, gentlemen,' said Macleod. 'Although, there's not a lot good about it. I hear that you're not going ahead with the tour application.'

'Well, how can we?' said Peters. 'I can't believe she did that. I can't believe that she actually killed people.'

'And clever with it,' said Ayres. 'So clever to not be caught on the first one, actually had an alibi. There's no wonder she was able to get away with the later ones. And then when the tour pressure came on . . .'

'The tour pressure came on and she kidnapped a child instead. She made it out that Pádraig O'Reilly committed suicide. Very dangerous and very clever woman,' said Macleod.

'Well,' said Cecil Ayres, 'It's not something I want to go through again. I think that might be me on the board. I just wished it hadn't have come during my time.'

Macleod watched the old man walk out of the room, his heart sullen. When the door had closed behind him, Macleod looked over at Peters.

'She did well, didn't she?' said Macleod. 'Having an alibi for that first one. I think it was the first one that inspired her.'

'What do you mean inspired her?' asked Peters. 'How do you inspire yourself with a killing?'

'Because she didn't do it,' said Macleod. 'She was not the killer of Sandy Mackintosh.'

Peters pulled a perplexed face, but then wandered over to the window. Macleod followed while Hope waited across the room.

'The knife was found on the links course, the bottom of the pond. I'm not sure that gets dredged very often, does it?' said Macleod. 'That's a detail you'd have to know.' The knife was also Spanish, Navaja, part of a martial art. It's a historical martial art though, and they don't practice it much these days. People who take part in historical re-enactments, however, have been known to learn some of it for the moves. I believe you've learnt it.

'Well, that's true, Inspector. I have indeed, but that's no crime. All I did was learn a few moves to show off to a crowd.'

'No, that's no crime, but there were two crimes, weren't there? When I saw you at the graveyard, it clicked. Also, your words. You talk about how things used to be. You talk about how you were inseparable from Sandy Mackintosh, the two families, you and your wife, he and his wife all the time. And there you were weeping at your wife's grave, weeping. I didn't hear the words you said to her, but when I walked away I heard you spit on her grave. It's funny; that doesn't happen very often,' said Macleod.

'There must have been some sort of righteous anger when Pádraig O'Reilly blotted his copybook. You exploded at it. When you've been hurt yourself, well then, you expressed the sympathy for his wife, as one who understands, I think it was

Sandy Mackintosh and your wife,' said Macleod. 'How long were they lovers?'

'She told me just before she died. Why didn't she take it to the grave? For most of our life when I knew him, the two of them were . . . well, he used to play in a foursome with her. They didn't have to practise. The new course was better for them for that. Previously they'd have to hurry their practising and then drive off somewhere but in the new course they could hide in bushes. Although, they must have been getting old for that. Why did she have to tell me though?'

'Told you right before she died, didn't she?' said Macleod. 'And there he was on the other side. Not only was he stopping your dreams of bringing the tour here, but he was also a reminder of her infidelity. A reminder of what she was.'

'Damned whore,' said the man bitterly. 'I loved that damned whore all of my life. Behind my back. We had kids, Inspector.'

'Sandy had to go then.'

'Tell me this, Inspector, how do you forgive somebody for a lifetime of deception? Wasn't a momentary indiscretion; it was all the time. Every lie to me, behind my back. And then I'm at the bar with him. We're off golfing together and he's laughing with me. All the time he's laughing behind my back, taking the one thing that's precious in my life and ruining it. How do you forgive that?'

'You can,' said Macleod. 'I do believe you can, but you couldn't. You acted quick. Your strokes, your cuts were clean. When Amy killed Orla Smith, it was butchery. No skill behind the blade, a total lack of knowing what she was doing but not you. You had practised the moves, over and over.'

'It's not the same though, do you know?' said Peters. 'Not the same when you do it yourself. You can practise but when

232

you see their face, when you slash across them and the pain and then you watch as the life disappears from them. Then I thought about what he was to me. That's why I set him up on the tee. That's Sandy's folly. You can't forgive that, Inspector. You can't forgive when they've done it in your face for so long.'

'I don't blame you for your anger,' said Macleod, 'but you killed a man. You killed the man in cold blood. You'll do time for that.' He turned and looked across the room. 'Your case,' he said to Hope.

Macleod got to the door and heard Hope arresting Andrew Peters. Macleod opened the door and returned back up to the office. Ten minutes later, Hope entered as well. Instead of going behind her desk, she walked over to where Macleod was sitting and perched on the end of a table. 'How much did you know and when?' she said. 'Were you going to tell me?'

'No, it might have skewed your view. I thought early on that there may have been more than one killer, but to inspire someone, to have done a killing so well, I'm not sure Amy Johnson even realised what it was about. I think she may have thought Andrew Peters was leading the way. Of course, his reaction outside of it was brilliant to her. How he kept a straight face. He was in fact deeply upset. He killed his friend, outside of his wife, probably his best friend, and she had cheated on him. You can forgive something like that,' said Macleod; 'you must be able to, but I don't blame him for not being able. Takes a heck of a strong person.'

'Well,' said Hope. 'I hope that won't look too bad on my record, only getting half the case solved.'

'Your arrest, you do the paperwork. One team, Hope. I've had plenty of pats on the back for stuff you guys have done. You've lifted me up and supported me. You take the credit on this one. Just be aware next time. It's hard when you take the reins fully. It's hard when you try and work out what's going on and it's not working out right, but you've got a job to do now,' said Macleod.

Hope looked at him puzzled.

'After-case party. Where are you going? I realise you may not be the party freak that I am, but you know, we still need to have one.'

'Paperwork done today, curry house tonight,' she said. 'What about it?' Hope shouted over to Clarissa. 'Curry house tonight?'

'Which curry house?' she said.

'That's never bothered you. You're not that deeply into your curries, are you?'

'She's worried about which one you're going to. I heard she's off on a buggy later on.'

Clarissa punched Ross on the shoulder. 'You can shut up about that,' she said, 'as can the rest of you. No remarks to him. You treat him nice.'

Macleod watched her scan the room, penetrating eyes and he began to smile. Clarissa left and he watched her go.

'What are you smiling at?' said Hope.

'See how defensive she was? She's keen on him. Really keen on him.'

'God help him,' said Hope.

'Absolutely,' said Macleod. 'May God help him indeed.'

Read on to discover the Patrick Smythe series!

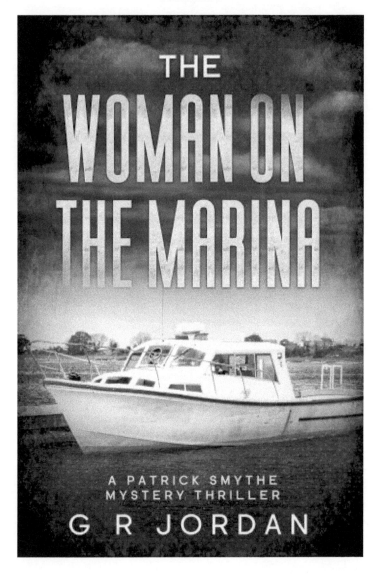

THE

WOMAN ON

THE MARINA

A PATRICK SMYTHE
MYSTERY THRILLER

G R JORDAN

Patrick Smythe is a former Northern Irish policeman who

after suffering an amputation after a bomb blast, takes to the sea between the west coast of Scotland and his homeland to ply his trade as a private investigator. Join Paddy as he tries to work to his own ethics while knowing how to bend the rules he once enforced. Working from his beloved motorboat 'Craigantlet', Paddy decides to rescue a drug mule in this short story from the pen of G R Jordan.

Join G R Jordan's monthly newsletter about forthcoming releases and special writings for his tribe of avid readers and then receive your free Patrick Smythe short story.

Go to https://bit.ly/PatrickSmythe for your Patrick Smythe journey to start!

About the Author

GR Jordan is a self-published author who finally decided at forty that in order to have an enjoyable lifestyle, his creative beast within would have to be unleashed. His books mirror that conflict in life where acts of decency contend with self-promotion, goodness stares in horror at evil, and kindness blindsides us when we at our worst. Corrupting our world with his parade of wondrous and horrific characters, he highlights everyday tensions with fresh eyes whilst taking his methodical, intelligent mainstays on a roller-coaster ride of dilemmas, all the while suffering the banter of their provocative sidekicks.

A graduate of Loughborough University where he masqueraded as a chemical engineer but ultimately played American football, Gary had worked at changing the shape of cereal flakes and pulled a pallet truck for a living. Watching vegetables freeze at -40'C was another career highlight and he was also one of the Scottish Highlands "blind" air traffic controllers.

These days he has graduated to answering a telephone to people in trouble before telephoning other people to sort it out.

Having flirted with most places in the UK, he is now based in the Isle of Lewis in Scotland where his free time is spent between raising a young family with his wife, writing, figuring out how to work a loom and caring for a small flock of chickens. Luckily, his writing is influenced by his varied work and life experience as the chickens have not been the poetical inspiration he had hoped for!

You can connect with me on:
Ⓖ https://grjordan.com
🅕 https://facebook.com/carpetlessleprechaun

Subscribe to my newsletter:
✉ https://bit.ly/PatrickSmythe

Also by G R Jordan

G R Jordan writes across multiple genres including crime, dark and action adventure fantasy, feel good fantasy, mystery thriller and horror fantasy. Below is a selection of his work. Whilst all books are available across online stores, signed copies are available at his personal shop.

The First Minister: Past Mistakes Trilogy #1
A cryptic note to a long-retired policeman. A clergyman stabbed by a masked figure in public. Can Macleod and McGrath find the story behind the panic as it becomes open season on the church?

When a note is delivered to a care home on the isle of Harris, it seems to be a joke in bad taste until the prediction comes true. As more notes are sent and clergy die, Macleod and his team have to open up a wall of silence regarding the reason for such hatred. In a trail that leads across all of Scotland, the DCI finds something more unpalatable than the murders before him.

A wall of silence can only be broken by blood!

Infiltrator (A Kirsten Stewart Thriller #10

Secrets being leaked from an overseas embassy. A mole too clever to be fooled by standard red herrings. Can Kirsten keep herself alive and find the mole before he discovers her cover?

Back in the pay of the British secret services, Kirsten must travel to South America where secrets are being passed through a mole known only as 'The Goldsmith'. But as Kirsten unearths the true nature of the information being passed, she finds herself in a race against time to stop a dirty bomb that goes right for the heart of British society.

The countdown has begun!

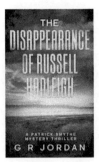

The Disappearance of Russell Hadleigh (Patrick Smythe Book 1)
https://grjordan.com/product/the-disappearance-of-russell-hadleigh
A retired judge fails to meet his golf partner. His wife calls for help while running a fantasy play ring. When Russians start co-opting into a fairly-traded clothing brand, can Paddy untangle the strands before the bodies start littering the golf course?

In his first full novel, Patrick Smythe, the single-armed former policeman, must infiltrate the golfing social scene to discover the fate of his client's husband. Assisted by a young starlet of the greens, Paddy tries to understand just who bears a grudge and who likes to play in the rough, culminating in a high stakes showdown where lives are hanging by the reaction of a moment. If you love pacey action, suspicious motives and devious characters, then Paddy Smythe operates amongst your kind of people.

Love is a matter of taste but money always demands more of its suitor.